PRAISE FOR SARA MESA

"With short, propulsive chapters, Sara Mesa creates an unforget-
table gothic landscape, centered on the mysterious and menacing
Wybrany College, that twists in ways that unsettle and thrill. In
Four by Four, Mesa's sentences are clear as glass, but when you look
through you will be terrified by what you see."
—Laura van den Berg, author of *The Third Hotel*

"The atmospheric unraveling of the mystery will keep you turning
the page; the ending will leave you stunned—Mesa's *Four by Four*
is a tautly written literary thriller that juxtaposes the innocence
of children with the fetish of control; a social parable that warns
against the silence of oppression and isolation through its disquiet-
ing, sparse prose."—Kelsey Westenberg, Seminary Co-op

"This is a linguistically precise, stylistically spare and emotionally
devastating look at the corrosive effect of abuse and power imbalance, perfect for fans of Shirley Jackson and Samanta Schweblin."
—Cindy Pauldine, Shelf Awareness, starred review

"*Bad Handwriting* is an achievement of the short form: subdued,
unpretentious, piercing, true."—*World Literature Today*

"Like Buñuel's *Exterminating Angel*, or even Bong Joon-ho's *Parasite*, the rich are left rotting in a swamp of their own design. . . . *Four by Four* is an uncomfortably real look into the absurd world of the bourgeoisie. It is so complex and layered that, to reach a full understanding, one may have to read it two or even three times. Not a single character, after all, is what they seem."
—Noelle McManus, *The Women's Review of Books*

". . . [I]n books like the successful *Bad Handwriting*, she is unafraid of letting the elements we sweep under the rug take center stage. Mesa urges her audience to meet the unlikeable head-on. In doing so, she allows us to see just where our reflections hide in the frightening world of reality."—Benjamin Woodard, *On the Seawall*

"The power in Mesa's work comes from the tension between the ease of her phrasing and the shock of its thought hitting your mind. If she added more, she'd limit our imagination. But the terse nature of her lines lets the idea slink from the page and burrow into our brain."
—Brian Wood, author of *Joytime Killbox*

"*Among the Hedges* is a daring, sympathetic novel about a friendship between two people whom society would prefer to keep apart."
—*Foreword Review*

"[Sara Mesa] deftly mixes immersive narration and relentless creepiness with incisive class commentary; by the novel's end, I was appalled both for its characters and for my own world."—Lily Meyer, NPR

"*Four by Four* is a masterclass in restraint and tension for both writers and translators."—Book Riot

"Mesa has an almost magical ability to write long sentences that seem short. Her stories use bluntness to devastating effect, both when it comes to the prose itself and in the way she develops characters. Very few authors are willing or able to inhabit protagonists as loathsome as some of [hers]. . . ."—*Astra Magazine*

"Stylistically, *Four by Four*'s narrative structure is both dazzling and dizzying, as its perfect pacing only enhances the metastasizing dread and disease. . . . Mesa exposes the thin veneer of venerability to be hiding something menacing and unforgivable—and *Four by Four* lays it bare for all the world to see."
—Jeremy Garber, Powell's Books

"Her keen eye for shifts in the balance of power is what makes [*Among the Hedges*] such an unsettling tour de force."
—*The Times Literary Supplement*

UN AMOR:
A NOVEL

SARA MESA

TRANSLATED BY KATIE WHITTEMORE

OPEN LETTER

LITERARY TRANSLATIONS FROM THE UNIVERSITY OF ROCHESTER

Originally published in Spanish as *Un Amor* by Anagrama
Copyright © 2020 by Sara Mesa
Translation copyright © 2023 by Katie Whittemore

Library of Congress Cataloging-in-Publication Data: Available

ISBN (pb): 978-1-948830-77-5
ISBN (ebook): 978-1-948830-90-4

This project is supported in part by an award from the New York State Council on the Arts with the support of the governor of New York and the New York State Legislature

This project is supported in part by a grant from Acción Cultural Española (AC/E), a state agency.

Printed on acid-free paper in the United States of America.

Cover Design by Alban Fischer

Open Letter is the University of Rochester's nonprofit, literary translation press:
Dewey Hall 1-219, Box 278968, Rochester, NY 14627

www.openletterbooks.org

UN AMOR:

A NOVEL

I

Nightfall is when the weight comes down on her, so heavy she has to sit to catch her breath.

Outside the silence isn't what she expected. It isn't real silence. There's a distant rumbling, like the sound of a highway, although the closest one is regional and three kilometers away. She hears crickets, too, and barking, a car horn, a neighbor rounding up his livestock.

The sea was nicer, but also more expensive. Out of her reach.

And what if she'd held on a little longer, saved a little more?

She'd rather not think. She closes her eyes, slowly sinks into the couch, half her body hanging off in an unnatural position that will soon give her a cramp if she doesn't move. She realizes this and stretches out as best she can. Dozes.

Better not to think, but still the thoughts come and slide through her, intertwining. She tries to let them go as soon as they appear, but they accumulate there, one thought on top of another. This effort, this drive to release them as quickly as they come, is itself a thought too intense for her brain.

When she gets the dog, it will be easier.

When she organizes her things and sets up her desk and spruces up the area around the house. When she waters and prunes—everything is so dry, so neglected. When it gets cool.

It will be much better when it cools.

The landlord lives in Petacas, a small town fifteen-minutes away. He shows up two hours later than they'd agreed. Nat is sweeping the porch when she hears the Jeep. She looks up, squints. The man has parked at the entrance to the property, in the middle of the road, and makes his way over, scuffling his feet. It's hot. It's noon and already the heat is intemperate.

He doesn't apologize for being late. He smiles, shaking his head. His lips are thin, his eyes sunken. His worn coverall is grease stained. It's hard to gauge how old he is. The wear and tear isn't to do with his age, but with his tired expression, the way he swings his arms and bows his knees as he walks. He stops in front of her, puts his hands on his hips, and looks around.

"Already getting started, eh? How was your night?"

"Fine. Mostly. Too many mosquitos."

"You've got a gadget there in the dresser drawer. One of those repeller things."

"Yeah, but it didn't have any liquid in it."

"Well, sorry, kid," he spreads his arms wide. "Life in the country, eh!"

Nat does not return his smile. A bead of sweat drips from her temple. She wipes it with the back of her hand and, in that gesture, finds the necessary strength to strike.

"The bedroom window doesn't close correctly, and the bathroom faucet is leaking. Not to mention how dirty everything is. It's a lot worse than I remember."

The landlord's smile turns cold, disappearing gradually from his face. His jaw tenses as he readies his response. Nat intuits that he is prone to anger and wishes she could backtrack. Arms crossed, the man contends that she came to see the house and was perfectly aware of its condition. It's her problem if she didn't pay attention to details, not his. He reminds her that he came down—twice—on the price. Lastly, he informs her that he will be taking care of all the necessary repairs himself. Nat doubts that's a good idea, but she doesn't argue. Nodding, she wipes away another bead of sweat.

"It's so hot."

"You going to blame me for that, too?"

The man turns and calls the dog that's been scrabbling in the dirt near the Jeep.

"How's this one?"

The dog hasn't lifted its head since it arrived. Skittish, it sniffs the ground, tracking like a hound. It's a long-legged, gray mutt with an elongated snout and rough coat. Its penis is slightly erect.

"Well, you like him or not?"

Nat stutters.

"I don't know. Is he a good dog?"

"Sure he's a good dog. He won't win any beauty contests, you can see for yourself, but you don't care, do you? Isn't that what you said, that you didn't care? He doesn't have fleas or anything bad. He's young, he's healthy. And he doesn't eat much, so you won't need to worry about that. He'll scrounge. He looks after himself."

"Okay," Nat says.

They go inside the house, review the contract, sign—she, with a careless scribble; he, ceremoniously, pressing the pen firmly to the paper. The landlord has only brought one copy, which he tucks away, assuring her that he'll get hers to her when he can. Doesn't matter, Nat thinks, the contract has no validity whatsoever, even the listed price isn't real. She doesn't bring up the problem of the window or the bathroom faucet again. Neither does he. He extends his hand theatrically, narrows his eyes as he looks at her.

"Better for us to get along now, isn't it."

The dog appears unfazed when the man returns to the Jeep and starts the engine. The animal stays in the front yard, pacing and sniffing the dry dirt. Nat calls to him, clucks her tongue and whistles, but he shows no sign of obeying.

The landlord didn't tell her the dog's name. If he even has one.

She'd be hard pressed to come up with a convincing answer if asked to explain what she was doing there. That's why she hedges when the time comes, babbling about a change of scenery.

"People must think you're crazy, right?"

The cashier smacks gum as she piles Nat's shopping on the counter. It's the only store in a few-mile radius, an un-

marked establishment where foodstuffs and hygiene products accumulate in a jumble. Shopping there is expensive and
the pickings are slim, but Nat is reluctant to take the car to
Petacas. She rummages in her wallet and counts out the bills
she needs.

The girl from the shop is in a chatty mood. Brazen, she
asks Nat all about her life, flustering her. The girl wishes she
could do what Nat's done, but the opposite, she says. Move to
Cárdenas, where stuff actually happens.

"Living here sucks. There aren't even any guys!"

She tells Nat that she used to go to high school in Petacas,
but she dropped out. She doesn't like studying, she's crap at
every subject. Now she helps out in the shop. Her mom gets
chronic migraines, and her dad also does some farming, so she
lends a hand at the store. But as soon as she turns eighteen,
she's out of there. She could be a cashier in Cárdenas, or a
nanny. She's good with kids. The few kids who ever make it to
La Escapa, she smiles.

"This place sucks," she repeats.

It's the girl who tells Nat about the people living in the
surrounding houses and farms. She tells her about the gypsy
family squatting in a dilapidated farmhouse, right near the
ramp for the highway. A bus picks up the kids every morning;
they're the only kids who live in La Escapa year-round. And
there's the old couple in the yellow house. The woman is some
kind of witch, the girl claims. She can predict the future and
read your mind.

"She's a little crazy, so it's creepy," the girl laughs.

She tells Nat about the hippie in the wooden house, and the guy they call "The German" even though he isn't from Germany, and Gordo's bar—though to call the storehouse where they serve up bottles of beer *a bar* is, she admits, a bit of an exaggeration. There are other people who come and go according to the rhythms of the countryside, dayworkers hired for two-week stints or just the day, but also whole families who have inherited houses they can't manage to sell and who live somewhere else half the year. But you never see women on their own. Not women Nat's age, she specifies.

"Old ladies don't count."

During the first days, Nat gets confused and mixes up all that information, partly because she'd listened absently, partly because she's in unfamiliar territory. La Escapa's borders are blurry, and even though there is a relatively compact cluster of small houses—where hers is located—other buildings are scattered farther off, some inhabited and others not. From the outside, Nat can't tell whether they're homes or barns, if there are people inside or just livestock. She loses her bearings on the dirt roads and if it weren't for the shop—which sometimes feels more familiar to her than the house she's rented and slept in for a week—as a point of reference, she'd feel lost. The area isn't even very pretty, although at sunset, when the edges soften and the light turns golden, she finds a kind of beauty she can cling to.

Nat takes her grocery bags and says goodbye to the girl. But before she exits the shop, she turns back and asks about the landlord. Does the girl know him? The girl purses her lips, shakes her head slowly. No, not really, she says. He's lived in Petacas for a long time.

"But I do remember seeing him around here when I was little. He always had a pack of dogs and a really bad temper. Then he got married, or got together with someone, and left. I guess his wife didn't want to live in La Escapa—can't blame her. This place is worse for girls. Even though Petacas is nothing special—I wouldn't want to live there either, no way."

She tries to play with the dog, tossing him an old ball she found in the woodpile. But instead of catching it and bringing it back, the dog limps away. When she crouches down next to him, putting herself on his level so he won't be afraid, he skulks off with his tail between his legs. The dog is a piece of work, she thinks, a real rotter. *Sieso*, they'd call him in the part of Spain she comes from. It seems a good a name as any—after all, she has to call him something. It certainly describes his surly nature. But Sieso is as inscrutable as he is unsociable. He hangs around, but it's like he wasn't there at all. Why should she have to settle for a dog like that? Even the little dog in the shop, an extremely anxious Chihuahua mix, is much nicer. All the dogs she meets on the roads—and there are tons of them—run over when she calls. A lot of them are looking to be fed, of course, but also to be pet; they are nosy and curious, wanting to know who this new girl in the neighborhood is. Sieso doesn't even seem interested in eating. If she feeds him, great, and if not, that's fine too. The landlord wasn't kidding:

11

the animal's upkeep is cheap. Sometimes Nat is ashamed of the aversion she feels toward the animal. She asked for a dog and here he is. Now she cannot—must not—say—or even think—that she doesn't want him.

One morning at the shop, she meets the hippie, as the girl called him. Now she languidly waits on them both, smoking a cigarette with no sense of urgency. The hippie is a little older than Nat, though he can't be more than forty. Tall and strong, his skin is weathered by the sun, his hands broad and cracked, his eyes hard but placid. He wears his hair long in a terrible cut and his beard is on the reddish side. Why the girl calls him "hippie" is something Nat can only guess. Maybe it's his long hair or because he is someone who, like Nat, comes from the city, a stranger, something incomprehensible for anyone who has lived in La Escapa since childhood and can only think of getting away. The truth is, the hippie has lived there a long time. He is, therefore, nothing novel, not like Nat. She observes him from the corner of her eye, his efficient movements, concise and confident. As she waits her turn, she pats the back of the dog he has brought with him. She's a chocolate Labrador, old but undeniably elegant. The dog wags her tail and noses Nat's crotch. The three of them laugh.

"What a good girl," Nat says.

The hippie nods and holds out his hand. Then he changes his mind, withdraws it and moves in to kiss her. Just one kiss on the cheek, which causes Nat to remain with her face tilted, waiting for the second kiss that doesn't come. He tells her his name: Píter. With an *i*, he specifies: P-í-t-e-r. At least that's how he likes to spell it, except when he's forced to write it officially. The less one writes one's real name, the better, he jokes. It's only good for signing checks at the bank, for those thieves.

"Natalia," she introduces herself.

Then comes the obligatory question: what is she doing in La Escapa? He's seen her out on the trails and also saw her tidying up the area around the house. Is she going to live there? Alone? Nat feels awkward. She would prefer that nobody watch her while she works, especially without her knowledge, which is inevitable because the boundaries of the property are marked only by fine wire mesh, denuded of vegetation. She tells him she's only staying a couple of months.

"I've seen the dog, too. You got him here, right?"

"How do you know?"

Píter confesses that he knows the animal. One of the landlord's many. That dog, in fact, is probably the worst of the lot. Her landlord will pick them up wherever, doesn't train them, doesn't vaccinate them, doesn't care for them in the slightest. He uses, then abandons, them. Did she ask for the dog? She can be sure the landlord has given her the most useless one he had.

Nat considers this and the man suggests she give the dog back. There's no reason to settle if he isn't what she wanted. The landlord isn't a good guy, he says, she's better off keeping her distance. He doesn't like to speak badly of anyone, he insists, but the landlord is another matter. Always thinking about how to scam people.

"I can get you a dog if you want."

The conversation leaves Nat uneasy. Sitting on her doorstep with a lukewarm bottle of beer—the fridge, too, is on the fritz—she watches Sieso sleeping beside the fence, stretched out in the sunshine. The flies loiter on his slightly swollen belly, where the marks of old wounds are visible.

The thought of returning him is deeply unsettling.

The house is a squat structure, single-story, with windows that are practically level with the ground and one bedroom with two single beds. Nat wanted the landlord to take away one of the beds—she won't need it—so she could set up a desk instead. She'd be fine with a plain board with four legs. She considers calling him but keeps putting it off. When she does see him— since she'll have to see him sooner or later—she will ask. Or hint. For the time being, she'll work without a desk, making do with the house's only table, which she moves against the wall because the place is gloomy and damp, even during the day. The kitchen—little more than a counter and stovetop—is so grim that she has to turn on the overhead light just to make a cup of coffee. Outside is different. Starting at daybreak, the sun beats down on the land, and working in the yard, even first thing in the morning, is exhausting. She tries hoeing rows to plant peppers, tomatoes, carrots, whatever grows fast and readily. She's read about how to do it. She's even seen a few videos that explain the process step by step, but once she's in the dirt, she's incapable of putting any of it into practice. She'll have to overcome her embarrassment and ask somebody. Maybe Píter.

In the evening, she sits down to translate for an hour or two. She never manages to concentrate. Maybe she requires a period of adaptation, she tells herself, no need to obsess yet. She takes walks around the surrounding countryside to clear her head. No matter how insistently she calls, Sieso refuses to go with her, and so she goes alone, listening to music on her earphones. When she sees another person approaching, she speeds up, even jogs a bit. She prefers to go unnoticed, not be forced to introduce herself or chat, even if that means pretending to exercise.

Cork oaks, holm oaks, and olive trees stud the drought-affected terrain. Rockrose, sticky and unassuming, are the only flowers to dot the land. The monotony of the fields is broken only by the mass of El Glauco, a low mountain of brush and shrub that looks as though it's been sketched in charcoal across a naked sky. Up on El Glauco, they say, you can still find foxes and wild boar, though the hunters who climb it only come back with strings of quail and rabbit on their belts. It's an eerie mountain, Nat thinks, quickly dismissing the thought. Why eerie? Glauco is an ugly name, certainly; she supposes it must come from the mountain's pale, wan color. The word *glauco* reminds her of a diseased eye, sick with conjunctivitis, or elderly eyes, glassy and red, almost tarnished. She realizes she is allowing herself to be influenced by the meaning of *glaucoma*. Coincidentally, in the book she is attempting to translate, the word *glauco* appears as an adjective attributed to the main character, the fearsome father who at one point directs an injurious imprecation to one of his sons, while fixing him—according to the text—with a glaucous gaze. At first, Nat thought it meant an eye infection, but later she understood that a glaucous gaze is simply an empty, inexpressive look, the kind in which the pupil appears dead, almost opaque. What, then, is the correct meaning? *Light green, blueish green, sickly, dim, distant?* She will have to orient the rest of the paragraph around the term she chooses. It would be like cheating to opt for a literal translation without understanding the genuine spirit of the sentence.

Despite all her walking and physical labor, she sleeps poorly at night. She doesn't dare open the windows. Not just because of the mosquitos, which still eat her alive despite all the products she bought. She's also found spiders and salamanders inside the house; horrified, she even discovered a centipede in one of her shoes. Another morning, she finds the kitchen overrun with ants because she left food out on the counter. She is besieged by flies during the day, both inside and outside the house. Can anything be done? she wonders. Or is this just the country, as her landlord would say? No matter how much she cleans, everything is dirty. She sweeps and sweeps but the dust comes in through cracks and accumulates in corners. If she at least had a fan for sleeping, she thinks, she could close the windows and everything would be more comfortable. She would wake up rested and with more energy to clean, translate, work in the garden—or rather, her plan for the garden. Asking the landlord for a fan doesn't even cross her mind.

She decides to go to Petacas to buy one. While she's at it, she thinks, she might as well get some tools. A hoe, buckets, a shovel, pruning shears, sieve, and a few other things. She can always figure out the exact names of what she needs.

She knows nothing about tools.

She is surprised by the activity in Petacas. It takes her a while to find parking; the layout of the roads is so chaotic and the signage so contradictory that once you enter the town, an unexpected detour can easily take you right out of it again. The houses are modest, their façades worse for the wear and mostly plain, but there are brick buildings, too, up to six stories tall, distributed arbitrarily here and there. The businesses are clustered around the main square; the town hall—an ostentatious building with large eaves and stained-glass windows—is surrounded by small bars and Chinese-owned bazaars. Nat buys a small fan at one of them. Then she wanders in search of a hardware store, reluctant to ask for directions. She is struck by the neglected appearance of the women, who have left the house with unkempt hair and slip-on sandals. Many of the men—even the old ones—are in sleeveless shirts. The few children she sees are unsupervised, licking popsicles, scampering, rolling on the ground. The people—men, women, kids—all of whom are loud and sloppy, look strangely alike. Inbreeding, Nat thinks. Her landlord is a perfect fit.

She worries about running into him, but it's Píter, not the landlord, whom she meets in the hardware store. She is happy to see him: someone she knows, someone friendly, someone smiling at her at last, coming over, what are you doing here, he asks. Nat shows him the box with the fan and he scowls. Why didn't she ask the landlord? It's his responsibility to keep the property in habitable condition. Not air conditioning, obviously, but a fan at least.

"Or you could have asked me. That's what neighbors are for."

Nat looks for an excuse. She's happy to buy one, she says. She'll take it with her when she leaves La Escape. Píter looks at her askance, pretending not to believe her.

"And what are you buying here? Tools to fix everything he left broken?"

Nat shakes her head.

"No. Stuff for the garden."

"You're planting a garden?"

"Well, just something basic . . . Peppers and eggplants, they're easy, I guess. I want to try, at least."

Píter takes her by the arm, steps closer.

"Don't buy anything," he whispers.

He tells her that he can lend her all the tools she needs. He says, too, that she might as well forget about a garden. Nothing's grown on her land in years; the soil is totally depleted; it would take days and days of hard work to get it into shape. If she insists—Nat hangs on that word, insists—he could lend her a hand, but he absolutely advises against it. Although he speaks smoothly, Píter's voice contains indisputable sureness, an expert's confidence. Nat nods, waits for him to finish his shopping. Cables, adaptors, screws, a pair of pliers: all very professional, very specific, nothing at all like the indefiniteness in which she operates.

Outside, Píter walks beside her at an athletic pace, straight but flexible. His way of moving is so elegant, so different from the people around them, that Nat is proud to be walking next to him, the sort of pride associated with feeling legitimate. The spell breaks when he points to the windows at the town hall.

"Pretty, aren't they? I made them."

Nat thinks the windows clash terribly with the building's exposed brick, but she is all praise: they suit it perfectly, she says. Píter looks at her appreciatively. Precisely, he says, that's what he seeks, for his work to befit its context.

"Petacas isn't the nicest place in the world, but—to the extent possible—one should strive to beautify one's surroundings, don't you think?"

"So, you're a . . ." Nat doesn't know what you call a person who makes stained-glass windows.

"A glazier? Yes. Well, more than a glazier. A glass and color artisan, you might say. Like, I don't just cover windows."

"Of course." Nat smiles.

They have a beer in one of the bars on the square. The beer is ice-cold and goes down easy. Píter observes her closely—too closely, she thinks—but his eyes are sweet and that softens her discomfort. The conversation returns to the landlord—that cheeky bastard, he repeats—the tools and her barren plot. He insists on lending her what she needs. Just a matter of tidying the yard, clearing space for a table and some lawn chairs, then planting a few oleander and yucca, or some succulents suitable for the harsh climate. There's a huge nursery near Petacas, very cheap. If she wants, one day they can go together. It seems her plans for a vegetable garden have been scrapped. She doesn't mention them again.

She devotes the following days to the exterior of the house. She rises early to avoid the heat, but even so, she sweats nonstop, and a grubby feeling stays with her all day. She scrubs the porch, scrapes, sands, and stains the pergola's wood floor and beams, prunes the withered branches running rampant, pulls weeds, removes bag after bag of trash—papers, dry leaves, metal, plastic, empty cans, more broken branches. The final result is basically a wide esplanade of cracked dirt. If the house were hers, she thinks, she would put in a lawn, and maybe the oleanders Píter recommended, they would create a natural fence to shield her from prying eyes, but that would be dumb, the house isn't hers, she's not going through all that effort for nothing.

One morning, the gypsy woman from the edge of the village pokes her head through the gate and asks if Nat wants any flowerpots.

"I got tons," she says.

She sells Nat a whole bunch for cheap. They're all old, but Nat isn't bothered by the chips on the ceramic pots or the mildew on the clay ones. There are two huge urns as well, and once they're scrubbed clean, they strike her as lovely. Since they're heavy, the gypsy's husband helps her carry them home, accompanied by two of their three sons. Nat likes that family. They're rowdy and good-natured, they don't go around complaining all day like the shopgirl. The kids pet Sieso and, for the first time, she sees the dog wag his tail and turn in a circle with an instinct to play.

"Just take some cuttings when you're out and about and you'll have the garden ready in no time," the gypsy husband says as he's leaving. "You don't need the nursery or nothing."

It's true. Nat picks plants from nearby houses, many of them empty, branches that poke through the fences around the properties and whose loss won't pose any problem to the owners. Nevertheless, when Píter finds out, he is annoyed. Was that really necessary? Didn't he tell her there was a nursery nearby, a super cheap one? He could have given her a bunch of cuttings himself, whole plants even. In fact, he gifts her a hardy cactus already budding with fuchsia flowers. Nat reluctantly places it by the door. It's a marvelous specimen and its simple presence draws all the attention.

The change to the yard is undeniable. The sprouts take root and grow by the day. Roberta, the old woman in the small yellow cottage, comes over to offer her enthusiastic congratulations. Nat feels immediately drawn to her. Why did the shopgirl call her a witch? If anything stands out about this woman, it's her sweetness. She must have been quite beautiful when young. Something of that beauty can be detected in the slender lines of her nose and mouth. Her eyes, though, are the most striking: dark, penetrating, warm. Her hair, fine and very white, spreads over her head like a light mist. The woman heaps praise on Nat's work. She says it's all very different since Nat arrived, and change—all change—is always good.

"Bad thing, stagnant water," she winks.

Nat realizes the woman thinks she's bought the house. No one in their right mind would go to all this trouble for a rented hovel.

Even a crazy old lady can see that.

Words another person wrote before her, words chosen with care, words selected from all the myriad possibilities and arranged in a singular fashion among infinite discarded combinations, these words impose themselves on her. If she wants to do her job well—and she does—she must take into account every one of those choices. Yet that line of thinking leads to exhaustion and paralysis. In dissecting language so conscientiously, she strips it of meaning. Each word becomes the enemy and translation the closest thing to a duel with both an earlier and better version of her text. Her slow progress is exasperating. Is it the heat, solitude, lack of confidence, fear? Or is it simply—and maybe she should just admit it—her ineptitude, her clumsiness?

Things with Sieso aren't going as she'd hoped, either. The dog refuses to enter the house, comes and goes as he pleases, ignores any and all rules. He doesn't trust enclosed spaces—obviously the result of some trauma—but Nat can't understand why he still won't trust her after so many days in her company. She remembers how he played with the gypsy kids and tries to pet him like they did—behind the ears, on his sides—but the dog acts defensive and flees, visibly on edge.

Lately, a concerto of barking and howling kicks up around two or three o'clock in the morning and fans out over several kilometers, as if all the dogs in La Escapa suddenly went mad at once. Nat wonders where they've come from, all those desperate dogs so full of aggression. They can't be the same animals she sees during the day, dozing or peaceably sniffing on the roadside. And if they are, why the nocturnal transformation? Why, all at once, are the gentle animals turning ferocious? And what if Sieso were to metamorphize, enter the fray, get hurt? Afraid he might run off, she decides she will tie him up. Perhaps her fear is overblown, misguided—as she'll think in the morning—since he always comes home safely at night, but the fear is real and indisputable.

Her plans had not included tying Sieso to a stake in the ground, but she can't think of how else to control him. Whenever she used to see a dog tied up, she'd thought it cruel and judged the owners harshly. Now she's doing the same thing, maybe for the same reasons. She promises herself the measure will be temporary, that once they form a bond, she'll let him run loose. Eventually, he'll end up sleeping in the house with her, to keep her company.

Píter, on the other hand, is not at all confident that Sieso will change. Every time he comes by to say hello, he looks at the animal sideways and tells her not to bother: the dog, he assures her, is damaged. He urges her to give him back. The longer she waits, the harder it'll be. When will she decide to listen to him? Nat thinks how Píter, contrary to his mild image and even his nickname, is always looking for conflict, at least when it comes to the landlord and pitting her against him. And it's not just the issue of the fan—as he continually reminds her—but the other problems around the house, and—especially—the dog. But if the landlord is such a bad person, what can they expect of Sieso, who lived with him and suffered who knows how many blows under his command. Píter himself told her about the landlord's attitude toward his animals: use then abandon them. If he's had Sieso since the dog was a pup, then it's what the animal has learned will be done with him, too.

Nat has the chance to change this, to turn the situation around, and for this reason alone—because such a chance exists and is in her hands—she refuses to give up.

One morning, she puts him in the car to take him to the vet in Petacas. It's a snap decision, and it turns out to be harder than she imagined. Sieso puts up a fight getting in the car, he spins around and watches her out the corner of his eye, suspicious. Finally, she manages to bait him with a piece of bacon and pushed him inside while he's preoccupied. Whispering to keep him calm, she settles him on a blanket in the back seat. Sieso stays, his legs stiff, panic in his eyes. He whines softly but remains strangely immobile. Throughout the drive, Nat checks on him in the rearview mirror. His mouth is open, panting, his head down, legs stiff, hackles up. The bacon lies untouched beside him. The animal is scared and she feels bad. Mostly she feels a desire for it to be over as quick as possible.

The vet clinic is on a dead-end street on the outskirts of Petacas. The place is empty. Not only are there no clients waiting, there's no waiting room. The vet, clearly a foreigner, receives her with irritation, as if she is intruding or interrupting him in the middle of another, much more important, task. He asks the dog's name as he puts on a pair of plastic gloves. Sieso, she says, embarrassed. When he raises an eyebrow, she hurries to clarify that it's an affectionate name, only half-serious, and that she'll change it in the future.

"Animals don't understand irony," he says. "It isn't good to go changing their names all the time."

His diagnosis is conclusive. Sieso has ear mites and worms. His limp is the result of an improperly healed back leg, broken at some point, maybe from being hit by a car. He is, moreover, malnourished and unchipped. Otherwise, the vet says, washing his hands, he's a young dog, and undoubtedly deserves a better life.

"Where are his papers? Is he current on his vaccinations?"

"I don't know. They didn't give me any papers."

The vet gives her a firm look.

"Can't you ask?"

"Yeah. I could, I guess."

Country people, he sighs. Nobody keeps track of these things. They're stupid and stubborn, and often cruel to the point of savagery. They brought a greyhound in the other day. The animal was torn to bits. Nothing he could do to save it. She simply cannot imagine the challenge of working in a place like Petacas. Like hitting a brick wall, he says, day after day.

25

Nat listens in silence. Her problem now is an economic one. To chip and deworm him, plus buy him good dog food, will cost a lot more than she'd budgeted for. And still, she fears, there's the question of his shots. But even taking into account the money she'll spend, the blow to her reserves, the most unpleasant part of the process, the most costly, will be interacting with the landlord.

She puts the dog bowl in the kitchen so Sieso will get used to coming inside. Sometimes she succeeds in getting him to stay a little longer, to lie down beside her. It's never for long, and he never seems entirely relaxed, but for Nat it's an accomplishment: having him there, close enough to touch. When she runs her palm over his back, she senses, under the fur, the agitation that still controls him, a continuous, pulsing current. He startles at the slightest noise or movement and is off like a shot. Then she has to earn his trust all over again.

That's exactly what happens one morning, when she sees him tense and jump up, whining softly, then go outside. A few seconds pass before Nat hears the Jeep put into park and footsteps on the gravel. It's the landlord, here to collect the rent. In cash, like they agreed. Like they agreed? Actually, she thinks angrily, she never agreed to anything. According to him, that's how they had to do it—if she wanted him to cut her a break, that is. No bank transfers or deposits, he'd decreed. She didn't care either way, did she? And now, all because she tried to avoid an argument, she's got him here in the house, after he rapped on the door and entered before Nat could respond. Before she even stands to greet him, he's looking around, evaluating the changes she's made, half-smile playing on his lips. Such a slight man, Nat thinks, so insignificant, yet he has the power to contaminate the house in just a few seconds. She takes out the rent money, hands it over to him in an envelope.

"You should let me know next time," she says. "I might not have been here."

"Bah, don't worry about that. If you aren't here one day, I'll come the next."

He's brought the bills, too. Electricity and gas, which are monthly, and the water, to be paid every three months. The fact that she's only been there a month is irrelevant. The house was unoccupied before she came, he says, so that bill—the water bill—is her sole responsibility. The amount is outrageous. Nat's hand trembles, just holding it.

"I already told you already that the faucet in the tub leaks. There's no way I've used this much water."

"What are you implying, that I should pay it?"

"I'm just saying it wasn't me. It's the faucet."

"Not the faucet's fault, girl. You're the one living here, aren't you? Then you should have fixed it."

She should have. Nat knows he is partly right, but she told him about it the first day and he did nothing, or rather, the solution he gave—fixing it himself—hadn't satisfied her. She could have asked someone else for help. Píter, for instance, though he would have criticized her giving-in. Or she could have simply called a plumber, like anyone else would do in her situation. In any case, she'd been avoiding it. She got used to the sound of constant dripping in the end. She turned her attention to other things. And now here she is, literally left holding the problem.

Fine, she says. She'll pay the bill with next month's rent, if that's okay with him. The landlord grunts an affirmative, not remotely grateful for her concession. Without another word, he leaves in a huff.

Only later does Nat remember that she never asked him about Sieso's shots, nor mentioned the bed she wants him to remove. It doesn't matter, she quickly tells herself, it's not that important. The mere risk of prolonging their encounter is so alarming that she would rather not to bring it up. She'll deal with it herself.

A plumber in Petacas agrees to come out to La Escapa the next day. That same morning, while she is still stretching in bed, Nat hears something in the bathroom. At first she thinks Sieso has gotten loose and come to look for her; still, she dresses quickly, heart racing, because the sounds are human sounds, not animal: footsteps, a bag dropping, faint throat-clearing, more footsteps on the tile. Nat shouts *who's there*, she peers, terrified, into the bathroom. She sees the landlord and cries out again. Fear at first, then indignation, and quickly, fear again. *What are you doing in here*, she shouts, repeating herself and on the edge of hysteria.

The landlord laughs, tells her to calm down.

"Easy, girl, it's me, it's fine."

He says he's come to fix the faucet. Needed fixing, didn't it? Hadn't she said so? He thought she wasn't home, or that she was still asleep. He didn't hear anything when he pulled up.

"But you can't come in without telling me first! You shouldn't even have a key! Who said you can open the door whenever you want?"

He laughs again.

"Don't get lawyerly with me, girl. I already said I thought you weren't home."

He explains that since the house was on his way, he decided to come by early. He has a few things to do in La Escapa later, and this way he doesn't waste the morning. He tells her he'll be done in a few minutes anyway, it's a simple repair, anyone could have fixed that faucet. Any man, he specifies, because she obviously hadn't been capable. Nat can't stop shouting. She insists, her voice distorted and strained, that he doesn't have permission to come inside like this, that he must never do it again. The landlord purses his lips, hardens his eyes.

"What, think I'm going to rape you or something?"

Scornfully, he gives her a once-over. Then he turns back to the tub, bends over, muttering, fussing with his tools. He says—under his breath, though Nat can hear him perfectly— that he's sick of women. The more you give them, he says, the worse they think they have it. Crazy, all of 'em. Neurotic. He continues to work and complain. Nat stands, frozen, in the doorway. Then she goes outside onto the porch and waits there for him to finish. She is still shaking.

"Done," he says a little while later. "See? Wasn't so big a deal."

He leaves without saying goodbye.

Still seated on the floor of the porch, Nat tries to contain her nerves, restrain herself from calling the police, or Píter, or whomever, hugging her knees until the tumult slowly gives way to a kind of calm. Even so, she forgets to notify the plumber, who turns up several hours later and, though there's nothing for him to fix, still charges her for the call.

"I rescheduled another customer to come. It's a pain to get here," he apologizes.

Nat makes no argument. It's true. This place, she thinks, is absolutely a pain.

She tells the vet Sieso hasn't had any of his shots. She'd rather lie and risk vaccinating him twice than have to speak to the landlord more than is necessary. Her only option is to open her wallet and get it over with. The procedure, however, turns out to be slower than anticipated—slower and more cruel. The second the needle gets close, Sieso suddenly wrests away. Nat is forced to pin him down while he is muzzled. She is startled by his viciousness, his curled lip and bared teeth. She fears this will be a step backward. Sieso might never forget her betrayal, the way she conspired to have him hurt.

She buys a harness, leash, plastic chew bones, and a training whistle. It will be complicated, transforming him into the peaceable and affectionate dog she needs, but she won't give up so easily. She will, in fact, take active steps to achieve it. That his evolution—arduous and minimal as it may be—should be validated gives her an intimate satisfaction, as if the dog's progress were also, indirectly, her own.

Still, his first afternoon out on the leash turns out to be exhausting. Sieso pulls and pants, almost strangling himself. Moments later, he sits down in the middle of the road and refuses to budge. Nat turns to drag him back, having only walked a few meters. Back at her house, she sees Píter at her front door, holding a box. When he sees her, he sets the box down and puts his hands on his hips.

"You're the stubbornest woman I've ever seen. What a ridiculous waste of your energy. What possessed you to put him on a leash? Dogs around here are never leashed."

"I was just trying to teach him. The vet recommended it. In case I have to bring him somewhere."

"And just where are you going to bring him? That animal will give you trouble everywhere."

Píter has brought her some vegetables he bought from the German. It's too much for just one person, he explains, but the German—very astute—always sells them like this, in big batches, so they don't rot on him. There are radishes, zucchini, cucumbers, tomatoes, and some bulbs Nat can't identify. The German? she asks, still wounded by Píter's comments about the dog. She seems to recall a guy, not that tall, with a mustache and glasses, awkward, dark and shy, a guy she's passed a few times on the road, a man who has hardly mumbled a hello and never met her eye.

"Oh. Thanks," she says flatly. "I don't know what I'll do with all of it."

Ratatouille? Chilled soup? Vegetable lasagna? There are a million recipes, Píter says. Why doesn't she quit wasting her time on the dog and make something for the two of them? He can contribute too, make a main course. They could have dinner at his place and he could show her his studio. Tomorrow. How's that sound?

Nat accepts. He's invited her to stop by too many times for her to keep putting it off. This time it's different, though. This time, it's a proper invitation: dinner, drinks, chat, all that implies. Nat isn't naïve, she knows the possible implications of Píter's invitation and, although something inside of her still resists—a subtle but persistent aversion—she needs to surrender. Ever since the landlord invaded her house, she has slept restlessly. She thinks she can hear the key turning in the lock, the door opening, footsteps approaching. She hasn't wanted to say anything to Píter because she knows what he'll say: that she should report the landlord to the police immediately. He will be stern, condemning her passivity and indolence. She would rather say nothing, keep it all to herself. And yet, it's not easy being so isolated; it's good to have a friend, otherwise she'll go crazy. She wonders if all she wants is friendship, or does she seek protection, too. Would she feel the same relief—or the same discomfort—if the invitation came from a woman? A female friend would do the trick, surely, but she wouldn't do much to alleviate Nat's defenseless feeling. In any case, she tells herself, Píter is the one expressing his desire to protect her. She just has to let him do it. She isn't asking for anything he isn't already willing to give her.

Píter's house is on the west side of La Escapa, some ten minutes from Nat's. It's a pretty wooden structure with a pitched roof, wide windows, and garden beds. The inside is cool and pleasant, and although the space is cluttered with objects, each appears to occupy a particular place and to have a precise function and purpose. When Nat steps inside, Píter's dog comes over to sniff at the pan in her hands.

"Stuffed zucchini," she announces.

Píter laughs loudly, taking her arm and leading her to the kitchen. A similar pan sits on the counter: the same dish. They laugh, the dog wags her tail and squeezes between them, looking for a pat. "My Funny Valentine" is playing, maybe the Chet Baker version, but Nat doesn't ask—she never asks those sorts of questions. Píter pours her a glass of wine and brings her down to the basement to show off his workshop. Everything there, too, is carefully organized; ready, even, for an exhibit: plans and sketches, glass fragments in baskets and boxes—classified by color—tools hung on the wall, a broad table with a half-finished windowpane and soldering irons suspended from the ceiling. Nat would prefer to poke around on her own, but she listens politely to Píter's explanations as he details, step by step, the process of stained-glass fabrication. A simple stained-glass window, he says, enhances any house, no matter how humble. Of course, if he's commissioned for something more formal, even institutional, he won't turn it down, but he prefers to work on a small scale, for regular people. Nat moves closer to study at the windowpane on the table. Lambs and doves dance around a leafy tree. The various shades of green used for the leaves create the impression of disorder, or imbalance. Nat isn't convinced that she likes it. Seen up close, the composition strikes her as conventional and rather unrefined.

"I was inspired by Chagall for this series. By the windows he made for the University of Hadassah, in Jerusalem. You know about them, I suppose, very famous . . ."

Nat doesn't have the faintest idea, but nods regardless. She turns to look at the wall, where other windows in the series are leaning, completed and ready to be installed. They're for a library, Peter explains, that's why he's put verses on them: by Pablo Neruda, Mario Benedetti, Wisława Szymborska. Nat reads them slowly, then asks:

"And you can make a living off of these?"

She regrets her words immediately. It's the sort of loaded question she hates being asked. Yet Píter doesn't seem bothered; quite the opposite, in fact. He answers gladly, with pride.

"Of course."

He spends very little on materials, he says. He uses mostly recycled glass. He finds the most valuable pieces in the trash, actually. He is committed to austerity as a way of life. His mottos are: throw nothing away; reuse all that you can; respect the Earth; go for minimal consumption, maximum depth.

"I have the feeling we're rather alike in that respect," he says, as a swift twinge of concern alights inside Nat's chest.

Her suspicions abate over dinner. Maybe it's the wine, but it's also Píter's affability; he proves to be warm and even witty, making her laugh like she hasn't in a long time. Nonetheless, she watches him from the corner of her eye as they clear the table and he opens another bottle of wine, finding something about him she just doesn't like, something that makes her hang back. It's not his physical appearance. In fact, his body is solid and attractive. His brawn is undoubtedly erotic. And he goes out of his way to please: he's charming, a good neighbor, knows about books, music, and movies, everything one assumes to be interesting in certain circles—her circle. So? Nat wonders why he lives alone, why he hasn't mentioned any women, dismissing the possibility that he might be gay. Then she takes the glass he offers her and smiles. She forces herself to brush off her prejudices.

They go outside into the yard to look at the stars. The night is clear and the Milky Way looms in the darkness, pure and immense. The tips of the blades of grass shine, bathed in the nocturnal light, swaying, ruffled by the wind. Píter's dog sits off to the side, drooling, pretty and regal in spite of her age. All three observe the sky in silence. So pretty, Nat murmurs as she simultaneously—perplexingly—thinks: my period. When the time comes, she can tell him that she has her period.

He turns toward her, scrutinizing her with a different kind of smile.

"Can I ask you something?"

"Of course."

"Why did you come to La Escapa?"

Nat falters. Hasn't she already answered that? Why does everyone assume she has a hidden motive? She doesn't answer, but drinks the last of her wine. Píter apologizes. He doesn't mean to be nosy, he says. She doesn't have to tell him anything if she doesn't want to, but, if she does want to talk, he'd be delighted to hear her story.

"I left my job," she says at last. "I couldn't take any more."

"What did you do?"

Nat demurs. She doesn't want to go into detail. It was just an office job, she says. Commercial translations, correspondence with foreign clients, stuff like that. Not badly paid work, but definitely a far cry from her interests. Píter lights a cigarette, squints with the first drag.

"Well, you're brave."

"Why?"

"Because nobody quits their job these days."

His praise irritates her. She might have accepted it under different circumstances, but now she's flooded with a desire to resist. Coming from Píter, the compliment sounds poisonous. Or maybe, it's her perception, blurred by alcohol, that makes her take it that way, twisted. No, she isn't brave, she counters. She didn't leave voluntarily. Not entirely. Does he want to know the real story? Píter leans in. Of course.

She stole something. She'd stolen, not out of necessity, but impulse. She never did comprehend why she did it. It wasn't for the thrill of the challenge, definitely not for greed. The object was just there and she simply took it. It belonged to one of the company's partners. To one of the partner's wives, to be precise, something valuable she left behind on a visit. Returning it got complicated later. Even if she'd wanted to—and of course she had—order was impossible to restore. She could return the stolen object, but not without consequences. She chose to stay quiet. She was caught in the end. They spoke to her privately, they behaved with discretion. She had always been a good employee, qualified and responsible. All they asked was why she'd done it, and she couldn't give them an answer. Well, they said, sometimes we don't know why we do what we do, right? Such benevolence raised her suspicions. She couldn't believe she was going to get off with a simple warning. Maybe someone had interceded on her behalf. Someone who would later make clear exactly what she owed them. Her absolution now had a price, and she wasn't sure she wanted to pay it. She was loathe to stay where they would always be looking over her shoulder, knowing she had something to hide. Where, if she kept her job, it was thanks to her superiors' compassion and generosity, and under the new terms of an unwritten contract.

Píter listens and nods, deeply concentrating on her story, but when Nat is finished, he simply repeats his initial compliment: she's brave, whatever she says. She's been brave enough to break with everything. Someone else in her position would have kept her head down, he's sure of it. She shouldn't feel guilty. Sometimes, certain mistakes lead us to the right thing, a change of course or even a revelation. Isn't it a good thing that she's here now, starting a new life?

They toast and drink, but a shadow has fallen, contaminating the air. A new life, Nat thinks, and immediately feels shame. Everything she has said is true; and yet, because of how she told it—her choice of words, cadence, pauses, and circumventions—her story is crowned with a halo of falseness she finds repellent. Her need to justify herself, she thinks, is pathetic.

Seeing her wilt, Píter kindly changes the subject, asks her about her current work, about the translation. It's her first assignment, she explains. Her first literary translation, that is. She's never done anything like it before. You could even say she's being tested. The publisher that offered her the job has faith in her abilities, but the project represents a qualitative leap, that's for sure. Commercial translation is straightforward and this . . . well, what she's aiming for is the essence, the very heart of language.

Píter is more interested in the book itself than in her theoretical digressions. What's it about, he asks. Is it a novel? Essay? What? It's impossible to explain, Nat says. There's no straightforward plot that I can sum up in a sentence or two. They're theatrical pieces, very short, almost schematic, philosophical in tone. The author didn't write them in her mother tongue, but in the language of the country where she lived in exile, so the prose is very rudimentary, flat even. At first Nat thought this would be an advantage, but it is revealing itself to be a challenge. Now she finds herself having to decipher whether every unexpected or ambiguous word is an error based on a faulty command of the language, or whether it's an intended effect, the result of intense deliberation. There's no way to know.

"Can you ask the author?"

Nat shakes her head, irked. The woman died, which is maybe for the best—she'll be spared from witnessing the mess Nat is making of her book.

Píter smiles, looks back up at the sky. A lovely profession, he says. Translation. Interesting and useful, he adds. Necessary. He sets aside his glass and, with a napkin, wipes his dog's mouth. The docile animal lets him do it, and in that placidity—and in Píter's manner—Nat observes great gentleness, but a type of gentleness that is also artificial, calculated. Sieso would never let anyone clean him like that. Maybe that's why Píter does it, to highlight the difference between the animals. When he's done, he refills Nat's glass. Fuzzily, she thinks: he's getting me drunk. A word begins to take shape—this—and then a complete sentence: this is how the charades begin.

Why doesn't Píter tell her anything about himself? Why is he nosing around, attempting to draw her out? Where does he get the authority to give her advice? Time for me to go, she announces, and on standing, realizes just how dizzy she is. She tries to dissimulate her wobbling as Píter takes her to the bathroom, where she stays a long time, until the alcohol's effects have dissipated somewhat.

It's very late when he offers to take her back to her house. He drops her at her front door and asks her if she'll be all right. Nat nods and thanks him. Píter brushes her cheek softly, bids her goodnight—get some rest, he says—and that's it. Nat is surprised, even disappointed. Wasn't he going to kiss her, or at least try? Wasn't he going to try to take her to bed? Isn't that the predictable thing, what's expected from a man? Why the Sam Cooke and the Miles Davis and all the wine, why the Milky Way? She had an excuse prepared for nothing. But then, would she have wanted anything different? No, of course not, but she doesn't want this either, the stumbling around in the entryway, the clumsy steps, the vertigo, the total solitude of the shut-up house. Nat lurches toward the bed and then hears something, a sound approaching from the shadows. She feels how her heart drops to the floor, until she realizes that it's Sieso, licking her shaky hand. It is the first time the dog has shown her any sign of affection, a greeting. Thrilled, she crouches down, cries, speaks to him.

"You scared me!"

She hugs him. His coarse fur gets in her nose and eyes, but still she hugs him, so tight that eventually Sieso wriggles away with a growl.

After that night, her relationship with Píter grows closer. Nat is at a disadvantage after having revealed certain things to him, but she isn't concerned by this asymmetry: she didn't tell him everything—not even close. His attitude toward her hasn't changed following her confidences. If anything, he is even more affable, more affectionate. They text each other throughout the day and Nat often visits him at home; she no longer needs an invitation, going over when she feels like it or is bored. Following her intuition, she steers clear of information she believes inconvenient to share. She doesn't tell him, for instance, about Sieso's gradual progress or her fear of the landlord. What for? Píter's tendency to insert himself into everything, his patronizing tone—the supposed voice of experience—because he's a man, because he's older, because he's been in La Escapa longer, because he's friends with all the people whose names Nat barely knows—doesn't seem serious enough to impede their friendship.

Paradoxically, what became obvious during dinner—that there is no sexual attraction between them—contributes to their closeness. And yet, Píter's disinterest sets off alarm bells for Nat: it signals that she is beginning to lose a power that she had, until now, unconsciously possessed. Like money, she thinks, erotic capital also imperceptibly erodes over time, we are only aware of it when it's gone, and she scrutinizes herself in the mirror with merciless eyes, inspecting the parts of her body or face where the flaw might reside. She has let herself go since arriving in La Escapa, it's true. Her hair is unkempt and coarse, the work clothes she wears do nothing for her, and instead of bronzing her skin, the hours spent in the sun have left it red and parched. But there must be something else. Something to do with age, or the *pressing* of time, not its passing.

She would rather not think about it. Like with so many other things, she sets the idea aside, quarantined.

Sometimes she has the feeling that the landlord has used his key again, entered the house in her absence. There is no demonstrable proof, nothing out of place, no evidence of his presence, but the mere possibility—a real possibility, as she has already seen—weighs heavy enough to cause distress. She forces herself to be rational. She must dispel her suspicions, not obsess. Yet all she has to do is close her eyes and relax her awareness and the landlord's specter waltzes in as a nightmare.

She has a recurring dream. In it, she discovers a window beside her bed, a new window appearing overnight. The exterior blinds are half closed and a pair of white curtains partially obscure the view outside. In what little she can see, she perceives an unfamiliar but perfectly realistic landscape. The scene isn't always the same: sometimes there are snow-capped mountains beneath an ashen sky, or a storm-tossed sea, or blocks of very tall buildings on the outskirts of a city, all with their lights on. When, fascinated, she tries to sit up for a better look, she finds that she is tied to the headboard—or the box frame or legs—with ribbons knotted at her wrists. They don't seem like much, the ribbons, but she is completely immobilized by them. She doesn't know who has tied her up, or when. She studies the knots pressing on her veins, the chafing on her skin, her fingers numb from lack of circulation. She is seized by fear. Just then, she hears the front door open. A man is coming inside, taking slow and scuffling steps that he makes no effort to conceal. Nat wonders where Sieso is, why he hasn't barked in warning. Without ever leaving the bed, she can somehow watch the man making his way through every room in the house—which is much larger than she'd thought and contains a multitude of rooms she didn't know were there: storage closets, attics, small rooms inside other rooms. She sees the man, the man's back, his bare, stalwart neck, watches as he penetrates every space, polluting it with his very presence. But she cannot see his face. The man approaches the side of the bed. Something in her throat turns spongy, muffling her scream. Nat is suffocating.

She wakes up sweaty, limbs heavy and gums parched. The night sounds mix with her still-confused senses: a horse's nervous whinny, the hoot of a brown owl, dense cricket song, and the dogs, always the dogs, their overlapping barks.

But worse are the noises she finds, even seeks, inside the house. Every day and night, dreaming or not. Creaks and squeaks, air whistling through the shutters, the hum of the fan, Sieso's toenails click-clacking on the old wooden porch, circling the stake. None of the sounds are associated with the landlord, but her guard is up. When he comes with the second month's bills, he knocks on the front door first. Nat's relief is so great that she pays without complaint. Better this way, she tells herself. Don't make any requests, wrap things up quick, and be rid of his face until the next month.

After so many days and so many walks, she knows all the little roads like the back of her hand, all the houses and who lives in them, but she can't shake the feeling that something evades her, things she can't see or understand. El Glauco's hulking form is omnipresent; no matter where she looks, there it is. Even when her back is turned, it stalks. I can't escape that mountain, she says to Píter. It's like I'm always being watched. But try to imagine La Escapa without El Glauco, he says: nothing but flatlands, no personality, just the same as everywhere else. It's difference that makes her uncomfortable, he says solemnly, and she realizes that they're talking about separate things, like they almost always do.

She is keenly drawn to one abandoned house. Someone has written GOD'S PUNISHMENT and also SHAME in big red letters on its crumbling walls. Píter tells her that a couple used to live there, a long time ago now, a brother and sister, who—according to the rumors—carried out an incestuous relationship. They fled to La Escapa from another village and stayed several years, reclusive and in a notable state of poverty—nobody would give them work—avoiding the insults and even attacks as best they could. Once, Píter says, somebody threw rocks through their windows, and another time, set fire to their shed. The man, who must have been about fifty, died from a sudden heart attack; a few days later, his sister, who was younger and appeared to be mentally handicapped, abandoned the house, leaving it exactly as it was. Almost immediately, the same people who had disavowed them with such disgust showed up to make off with anything useful. Everything else they maliciously destroyed in a big bonfire. The graffiti was added later.

But all of that happened ages ago, Píter rushes to add. It's a kind of urban legend. He didn't even live here back then, he's just recounting what he was told. She shouldn't get a bad impression of La Escapa, things have changed a lot since then, people are increasingly more tolerant, more civilized. If that

44

were true, Nat thinks, someone would have bothered to scrub the graffiti off. The words still there for all to see strike her as some kind of reminder. A warning, even.

She can spend whole days roaming and, except for work crews, meet almost nobody: just the gypsy collecting scrap metal or running errands, Joaquín—Roberta's husband—or the German, driving his van back and forth to Petacas, presumably to sell vegetables from his garden. If it weren't for Píter, she might not speak to anyone for days. Now that she's not a novelty, not even the shopgirl takes an interest in her. She simply rings up Nat's shopping, eyes glued to the TV mounted in the corner. Her boredom contains a whiff of despair. Nat watches her crack her knuckles, lost in thought, humming under her breath. Her still-adolescent face holds the template for what she'll be like at fifty or sixty, when she's plagued by the same migraines as her mother. Nat would like to be kind to her, but can think of nothing to say.

Sometimes she goes with Píter to Gordo's bar, a storehouse with an asbestos ceiling, lit by a single bulb emanating blue-tinged light. They drink bottles of beer with the men who stop in—farmers and bricklayers, mostly—people who discuss subjects to which Nat has nothing to add. Píter chats with them easily, even though she gets the impression that he's acting, intentionally getting down on their level. Sometimes Gordo charges extra, sometimes he doesn't charge at all, and no one's allowed to argue. There's always a hint of aggression, of provocation, in the way he jokes with his customers. They all laugh it off. Nat does, too. She would never go there alone, but with Píter it's different.

Weekends are livelier. The house next to Nat's, nicknamed The Cottage—as seen on the colorful sign at the gate—is occupied by a young couple with two small children—a boy and girl—who spend the day out in the yard, shouting to each other as if it were the most natural—and only—way to communicate. The woman, slim and chatty, seems welcoming, although she looks at Nat skeptically; maybe she doesn't quite understand what Nat's doing there alone, in that dreary, ill-equipped house, with that unfriendly dog. Píter, a long-time friend of the couple, made their upstairs windows, which lend the inside of the house a warm quality, a reddish or orange-tinged hue, depending on the angle of the sunlight. The neighbor woman tells Nat that she inherited The Cottage unexpectedly from a great-aunt. They tried to sell it but had no luck, nobody wanted to buy such a dark, dingy place. Instead, she says with a sigh of resignation, they capitalized on its potential, did some renovations so the kids could at least enjoy time outdoors. Her husband, the more enthusiastic of the two, mows the lawn with exacting regularity and amuses himself building playhouses and swing sets for their kids.

Nat is grateful when Monday comes and she can relax again.

One Sunday, the neighbors organize a barbecue and invite lots of people, almost all of them city friends who come to La Escapa expressly for the party. Nat and Píter are also invited. Nat wants to go, but once there she keeps shyly to herself, drinking and observing the others from a corner. She's not entirely sure why many of the guests walk around the yard in their bathing suits. It makes no sense, she thinks, since they don't have a pool, not even an inflatable one, just a garden hose they use to cool off or play with, like little kids. It's almost obscene: an immodest parade of imperfect bodies, half-naked and wet. They talk seamlessly about gastronomy and politics, sometimes about both topics at once. They pretend to be well-informed, which makes Nat withdraw even further. Some of the guests come over to chat, to ask about her life. They're curious about her presence in La Escapa, for which there is no obvious justification. Others think she's Píter's new girlfriend and behave accordingly, referring to them as *you guys*, which she doesn't bother to correct. All seem to find the idea of a retreat to the countryside, varnished with a romantic sheen, quite appealing. Nat wishes she could say that she's only there because it was the cheapest place she found.

Later, she finds the neighbor woman's eyes fixed on her from across the yard.

"I fear she's quite jealous," Píter whispers confidentially. "Her husband won't stop talking about you. Haven't you noticed?"

She had. The husband is the one who took it upon himself to introduce her to their friends—pride in his voice when he said her name—the one who insists on emphasizing particular details—that she's worked hard to fix up the house, that she's rescued a street dog, that she's a translator—the one who makes sure she always has a drink. A perfect host, but at the expense of his other guests. So all is not lost, Nat thinks. Her gratification, however, includes a measure of mockery. This is how it always is; she can't help but see it from the outside: a male on the hunt for new prey to fall at his feet, the penetrating gaze, willfully seductive, but the man's humped back, and his flat feet, the ridiculous bald spot when he turns around. She is amused. How absurd some men are.

On another day, Píter encourages her to participate in a local residents' meeting; not everyone from La Escapa will be there, but she should go, her opinion counts. What kind of meeting? Nat asks cautiously. She is irritated by the obligation couched in Píter's suggestion, and she isn't entirely sure about her role as a resident, she considers herself a newcomer, without voice or vote. La Escapa is a godforsaken parish, Píter explains, despite having a village mayor, who is—just imagine—the shop owner, a man who enjoys his power more than he lets on. Be that as it may, his authority isn't of much use: the rest of them must also step up and demand that the Petacas town hall—La Escapa's genuine administrative oversight—do something. Oddly enough, the people behind the meeting are the owners of The Cottage, Píter himself, and a few others from the new batch—that's his expression, *the new batch*. People who want to improve things. But what things, Nat asks, what things.

"You don't look very enthused."

"It's not that. I just don't know what good I'd do at the meeting. I'm just a renter, my landlord should be there."

"Your landlord doesn't care about the issues. You know what he's like."

She does. And she knows that Píter is partly right, even though that's hard for her to admit. He mentions the need to improve trash collection, the poor lighting on the roads—so treacherous at night—and the danger posed to car tires by all those potholes and dips.

"Your tires too, right?"

She nods: hers too. Ultimately, she agrees to go.

They hold the meeting in the shop. On arriving, Nat is surprised to see that they almost don't fit, although, as Píter had presaged, not all residents are in attendance. The gypsies, for instance, aren't present—Nat senses that for some, they represent as big a problem as the potholes—and neither is Gordo, who apparently doesn't get along with the shop owner—they want to kill each other, Píter whispers. Old Joaquín has come with Roberta, possibly because he doesn't have anybody to stay with her. The old woman isn't having her best day. Halfway through the meeting, she begins to speak incoherently in a brittle voice. Even though her speech is perfectly articulate, she uses learned words, seemingly unconnected, words with limited meanings, like *manatee*, *wetland*, *turbidity*, and *gland*. Nat recalls that those exact words appeared a film that aired on TV at midday. It was a tremendously boring documentary about the Antilles which must have caught the old woman's attention, disorienting her, because her manner of speaking contains a desperate, questioning timbre: what does all of this mean, she seems to say, why are they arguing about things she doesn't understand—things like *sidewalks, streetlights, dumpsters*—as if parading through her head are oceanic images and disjointed words.

Joaquín simply waits while his wife speaks, showing no hint of embarrassment, confident that the others will do the same—wait, resigned and courteous—but Nat senses the impatience, the glances, the throat-clearings. Píter smiles condescendingly, the couple from The Cottage whisper between themselves, the shop owner makes a face. Only the German remains unperturbed as he leans against some boxes of tin cans, head down, looking at his boots, which he slowly taps from side to side. Nat focuses on him. Why has he come to the meeting, as solitary and independent as he seems to be? Nat doesn't know why they call him that, *the German*, since he isn't German and doesn't look how one assumes a German would look, based on the caricature—a stereotype, of course—of a tall, blond, strong Teutonic figure. No, the man is small and dark, his hair is thinning, hairline receding. His nose is broad and ugly, his mustache droops, and the glasses he wears for nearsightedness don't make him look exotic, but utterly local instead. *The German* must be a nickname, just like Píter is *the hippie* and Roberta *the witch*. It's normal for people in small villages to have nicknames, right? Nat wonders if they've given her one, too. She's not sure she wants to know.

She finds a small snake coiled in the woodpile. A snub-nosed adder, with an insolent snout and focused scowl. Nat jumps back. She'd heard as a girl that their venom is fatal, that it can kill a man in half an hour. She has to get rid of it right away, but she's afraid it will slither toward her if she attempts to kill it. Besides, how would she do it? The thought of whacking it with a stick is repellent. She goes in search of aid. It isn't easy to find someone willing to lend her a hand. Píter is in Petacas and the bricklayers tell her they have a big job on that day. One man promises to come by when they finish up, but Nat can't wait. She finally manages to get the gypsy. Not only does he not object, but he comes quickly and readily, rolling up his sleeves. The adder hasn't moved. Sluggish under the sun beating down on the logs, the reptile is motionless but expectant, as if it anticipated the danger, watching them out the corner of its golden eye, its terrifying, vertical pupil. The gypsy uses a rock to smash it to death. Blood glistens on its mangled scales and the sight makes Nat feel sick. Relief, however, outweighs her disgust. She opens her wallet, looking for something to give the gypsy, but he holds up his hand, reassuring and perhaps slightly offended.

"Oh knock it off. I've killed plenty of these things . . . if they paid me every time, I'd have an Audi and a three-story chalet."

Píter will later say that she shouldn't have killed it. Snub-nosed adders aren't poisonous, that's nothing but an old wives' tale. Prejudices and unsubstantiated fears, that's how it goes, he says, shaking his head sadly. Does she really think a snake hardly a half-meter long would waste its venom, its rare, precious venom, on a human? No, a viper like that never attacks, not unless someone antagonizes it the way they had.

"So, what should I have done?" Nat asks.

"Nothing. Leave it alone. Or pick it up carefully and move it somewhere else. They were here before us, weren't they?"

Nat concedes that he's right—what choice does she have—but she thinks: even a common adder has preemptive rights over her land. No matter how much time passes, she will always be an interloper.

One night, the wind changes direction and the temperature drops. Nat is reading on the porch; first she gets a cardigan, then goes inside, still too chilly. Fat, hot raindrops promptly begin to fall and within a few minutes the downpour starts, raising a new, encouraging scent from the wet earth. Nat is as happy as a child. She feels like she's made it to the end of a phase, the first and most challenging, and that the rain marks the beginning of a new—and more promising—stage. But her joy is short-lived: just as long as it takes for the leaks and a swiftly widening puddle to appear. Nat runs for buckets; when she returns, hair and clothes soaked through, mud has already started forming inside the house. Incredible, she thinks. What does one do in these situations? And how hadn't she noticed before? Hadn't she seen the yellow stains on the ceiling a thousand times? What did she think they were? She spends half the night emptying buckets and putting them back out, until the storm wanes and she can lie down to rest. She sleeps in intervals, afraid the rain will start up again, knowing that, this time, she'll have no choice but to call the landlord. But the sky is radiant in the morning, not a trace of clouds. Can she put the call off? At least until the next time he comes with the bills? With any luck, it won't rain again before then; better to wait, not wake the dragon ahead of time. She knows she's making excuses, avoiding the problem, but she tells herself that they aren't really excuses, they are actual facts: the sky doesn't threaten more rain, it was just a passing August rainstorm, nothing to worry about for now.

Her forecast is correct: no drops fall over the coming days. She can almost manage to forget the issue, but not quite. Whenever she looks up, she is confronted by the stains, which look like limescale or urine and gross her out. When the month ends and the landlord shows up in his grubby overalls, Nat shows him the stains. He narrows his eyes to inspect them. She tells him what happened the night of the downpour, about the puddles and buckets. She explains that this is why the wood floor is rotting. This is irrefutable proof, she thinks. He cannot deny the evidence.

"Well, girl, it doesn't rain like that every day."

"Not every day, no. But it could happen again. I mean, it'll definitely rain this fall, right? Maybe not as hard, but the leaks are there and . . ." She falters. "The floor is getting ruined . . ."

The landlord looks at her breasts as she speaks. He's doing it on purpose, Nat thinks. To destabilize her, she thinks. Humiliate her. Lip curling, he says the rotting floor isn't her problem. Not her house, is it? She's just a renter, he repeats, a renter who has done nothing but complain ever since she arrived.

"What do you want me to do? You think the shitty rent you pay is enough for me to get bogged down in a bunch of home improvements?"

Nat, furious, is incapable of expressing her anger. She wants to be forceful. Instead, she just sounds hesitant and scared.

"So the next time it pours, I'm just supposed to put out buckets?"

"Exactly!"

He points a finger at her and she weakens. Her throat burns, a scorching sensation that reaches her eyeballs. Is she going to cry? She cannot let that happen. She must contain the urge, no matter what.

"I think . . . all of this just isn't . . . I don't think this is normal."

"No? Don't think it's normal, do you? And just what do you think is normal, girl? Coming out to the middle of the country and expecting your cushy city comforts?"

He starts to talk about women plural, throwing his arms around and pacing in circles.

"You women are all the same. You think the country is starry skies at night and little lambs bleating in the morning. Then you harp about the mosquitos, the rain, the weeds. Look, I already brought the price way down. Did I bring it down or not? Or don't you remember now? When you've had a problem, haven't I fixed it? Didn't I fix the faucet? Oh, you thought that was horrible, too. Can't understand you women. Look, I got more important things to do. Give me my money and get off my back."

Nat pays him and he leaves, slamming the door behind him. She cries then, full of rage because she cannot understand what it is about the landlord that is so terrifying. A rude, small-minded man with no actual power over her. Is he not clearly inferior? Uneducated, dirty, and poor, what damage can he do? Why does he have such an effect on her? She cries and, simultaneously, tries to convince herself that maybe there won't be any more leaks, maybe putting out a few buckets when it rains is fine, maybe that was an unusual storm, maybe it's not really that big of a deal, maybe she can hold out for a few months. It isn't her house, after all, she'll end up moving out sooner or later. In the meantime, it's better to be chill, not stress, not allow herself to get upset. This is how she will defeat him, how she will stay on top.

But the stains continue to speak for themselves. This time, it's the German who sees them when he comes around to offer her a crate of vegetables. He sets the crate down in the entryway and stops before the ruined floorboards. He looks up and examines the ceiling.

"You've got leaks."

He has an odd way of speaking, crowding his syllables, like he's in a rush or being brusque. Without meeting her eye, he asks for a chair and climbs up for a closer look. Nat notices his boots—sturdy and worn, the same pair he was wearing at the meeting—as he explains the cause of the problem.

"Looks like it's been like this a long time. There are probably a decent number of broken tiles up there. You'd need to check and see if they can be fixed, but I doubt it. When the leaks are superficial, you can just cover the tiles with bitumen or lime, but I'm afraid this is more complicated. What'd your landlord say?"

"That the roof only leaks when there's heavy rain. That it's not his problem. That he won't do anything."

The German climbs off the chair, shakes his head.

"Whenever it rains, even just a sprinkle, this will all flood again. I could fix it for you."

Nat is grateful that he doesn't comment on the landlord's position. She likes that he doesn't judge her, that he doesn't deem the situation fair or unfair, or urge her to argue or defend her position. The German sticks to the facts, views the situation head-on, abstaining from his own interpretation. It is exactly this attitude that gives her license to vent and complain.

"It's ridiculous that I have to fix it. He should do it, right? It's his house."

"Yeah. His house, but your problem. I can help you, seriously. I know how to fix it."

To prove it, he describes the process in detail: first, they need to evaluate the extent of the damage; then, get similar tiles and retile the affected area. Finally, channel the runoff with either grating or gutters so it doesn't happen again; they'd see about that later. But they're not friends, Nat thinks. She will have to pay him. And how much might something like that cost? She doesn't have much money, but neither will she accept any favors. Not that she doesn't trust him, but she doesn't want to owe him anything.

"I don't know if I can afford it," she says.

The German is silent. She suspects he's about to offer to do it for free. But after a few seconds, he says he understands. He can't give her an estimate for how much it will cost before he starts. He doesn't want to fix one problem for her and cause another. He shrugs and, for the first time, looks at her. There's no disappointment in his eyes. Or resignation. Just hints of timidity and kindness, maybe a bit of embarrassment. It could be that he's also short on cash and saw a chance to earn a little extra income. He seems honest to Nat, but rough around the edges. All she can do is cross her fingers in hopes that it doesn't rain and buy bigger buckets just in case. She pays and thanks him for the vegetables, then walks him outside.

Afterward, Nat will remember in meticulous detail what is to happen just two hours later. She will need to fix the details in place, not forget any of it, prevent it from being altered, adulterated, or disguised by her memory.

In her recollection, a word—*droit*—will echo, and a phrase—*le droit de sauver*—from a dialogue she was translating when it happened. You do not have the right to save whomever you want, one of the characters protests, and the other replies: It is not a right, it is a duty!

Nat is typing those exact words when she hears someone call her name. She stands and goes outside and it's him, the German, waiting outside the gate, even though it's been open since he left. She notices that he's changed clothes: the faded gray pants for a different pair, clean and blue, the black T-shirt advertising a mechanic's shop for a beige button-down so threadbare it's practically see-through. He doesn't smile, but he isn't serious either. Rather, he gives the impression of being very focused on something, something he's about to do or say and which doesn't seem to relate to Nat directly. It occurs to her that maybe he's forgotten something, or maybe she paid him the wrong amount for the vegetables, or maybe he's going to offer to fix the leaks for free after all, as she'd thought. His glance up at the roof confirms the third option. Predictable, she thinks, although she never could have foreseen what would come next.

"I don't want you to get mad," he says.

He stops there, studying the roof, squinting in the sunlight. Sieso approaches him slowly, sniffs his pant legs.

"Mad? Why would I get mad?"

He takes his time to find the words, but the delay doesn't appear to suggest discomfort with his message, but rather uncertainty about the use of language itself. Waiting for him to speak, Nat is intrigued, albeit slightly indifferent, as if what he was about to say—or propose, since it's obviously a proposal—didn't concern her.

"I guess you have the right to get mad. It's a risk I'm taking."

It's not a right, it's a duty! Nat thinks, but she smiles, encouraging him to speak.

"Come on, just say it, it's fine."

He says it. He says he's been alone a long time. A long time without a woman, he specifies. Living in La Escapa doesn't help. Neither does having a personality like his, cut off and reserved—he doesn't use those adjectives, though: he says, simply, *a personality like mine.* It's not like he's unhappy. He's not sad or depressed, that's not it. But the fact is that men have certain needs. His voice cracks a bit, but he steadies it right away. He's not that young anymore, he continues. Some ten or twelve years older than she is—he looks her over, appraising her. He doesn't feel old, but he also doesn't have the energy to go picking up women. He smiles, embarrassed, and Nat senses that it's not because of what he means, but the expression *pick up*—so euphemistic and antiquated, out of place. To meet women, he corrects himself. His smile fades. He doesn't want to resort to prostitutes; the ones in Petacas are horrible, he says, all of that completely turns him off. She nods mechanically.

It's very simple, really, the German continues. Or it should be. Even though men and women rarely think about it that way. No one dares to talk openly. The usual—or common—thing is to have ulterior motives. He thinks that with her, maybe he can cut right to the chase. It's just an intuition he has; maybe she'll misinterpret him and get offended, or maybe she'll interpret him correctly and still be offended. He doesn't know her well enough to anticipate her reaction; the only way to know is to just throw it out there. He waits a few seconds, searching her face.

"I can fix your roof, if you'll let me enter you a little while."

Nat will repeat these words to herself, over and over, until she fears she's made them up. He doesn't say *in exchange for sleeping with you*. He certainly doesn't use any other expression—more or less offensive—meaning something similar. He says *let him enter*. Not just *enter her* but that she *let him enter*.

An odd way to put it, and not the result of a deficient command of the language—he isn't German, after all! Let him enter, she repeats to herself. A little while, he said. *A little while.* Nat blinks. She needs to hear more, or perhaps hear it again, in order to understand. But his posture—the loose arms, legs apart, the humble, evasive eyes—seems to indicate that he is all done speaking and is now, quite simply, waiting for her reply.

"And how would that be, exactly?"

The German looks at her for a moment and tries to smile, but the expression is closer to a wince. Of relief? Of satisfaction, because she isn't angry? Nat wouldn't possibly know how to read it. Just once, he specifies. A little while, he repeats. The minimum, he says next.

"I won't hound you. I don't want to bother you. You're not a prostitute. I don't want you to think that I take you for one. It's just—" He hesitates. "I'd like to enter you for a little while. Simple as that. You lie down and I'll be done quick. That's it. I haven't been with a woman in a long time. My body needs it. I thought I could ask you."

Nat will later remember those words, too. The coolness of his statements, so short and direct. His concision. He could have said what people usually say in those situations. He could have said, for instance, that he liked Nat, that he was attracted to her, that he was risking such a request because he could barely resist her. But those last words—*I thought I could ask you*—mean nothing. He isn't asking Nat because he likes her, but because he thought he could ask her. So, whom can he not ask then? Whom doesn't he ask because—he believes—he cannot?

Nat reacts from a place of subtle but instinctual irritation, as well as impatience. The sense lasts but an instant, but is a deciding factor in her refusal, which springs from her lips, curt and direct, almost catching her off guard.

"Thanks, but no."

Okay, he says, and calmly makes to leave. He doesn't press her, but he doesn't apologize, either. Nat says goodbye as if, in effect, nothing strange had taken place.

Yet once back at her desk, she is unable to resume her work.

It will take several days before she is able.

II

It rains. Not a heavy rain, but gentle and steady, no peaks or troughs. It starts at midnight. Nat makes Sieso come inside, sets out the buckets, and stays alert to empty them before they overflow. The floorboards emanate a damp, clinging heat that makes her drowsy. She sinks sluggishly into an elaborate dream, a dream that continues after each interruption, never breaking off entirely. In this dream, Sieso has run off and she must go after him, but she's barefoot and the only shoes on hand are a pair of sturdy leather boots, like the German's. They are not appropriate footwear; the boots are so heavy she can barely lift her feet off the ground, can barely move. No matter how desperate she is, no matter how she hurries, she loses sight of the dog and only hears his increasingly weak whines. When she wakes, she realizes Sieso's whining was real and had entered her dream. But the boots? Were they real? Real or not, she thinks, they are not the solution to her problem.

The rain, and the revelation, disappear with the dawn. Nat studies the sky. Dense black storm clouds are amassing over

El Glauco; it won't be long before it rains again. But at the moment, in full daylight, she is calm. The leaks, she thinks, aren't such a big deal. She just has to replace the buckets when required; surely, there are people living in worse conditions who still get on with life, uncomplaining. The German's offer, his voice—his voice making the offer—still echoes in her head, but she isn't concerned. The German is in her memory just like he was on her doorstep a few days ago, speaking with surprising serenity. She will deal with it the same way. Dispassionately.

The bad weather will continue throughout the week, though it won't ever become unmanageable. It rains and stops, rains and stops, a tranquil rhythm, good for the crops. Even so, the leaks persist because there's no time for the roof to dry out between downpours. Nat spends hours and hours minding the buckets, she can hardly leave the house except to buy the bare necessities. The days pass and her fatigue grows. She watches the sky with discouragement. A growing angst coalesces within.

One noontime, when the rain lets up and a few breaks in the clouds are visible on the horizon, she leaves the house to stretch her legs. Sieso follows her to the gate, where he stands, unmoving, despite her persistent calling.

"Stay there, then," she snaps. "Your choice."

The dog watches her walk away down the road. Though the air has cooled, Nat is dressed for summer in a simple pair of shorts and a cotton T-shirt. She crosses her arms to protect herself from the chill and presses on into the headwind. She passes Píter's, barely glancing in its direction. She strides ahead almost mechanically, although she would never be so naïve as to deny that she knows perfectly well where she's going. She knows, all right, but not why or what for, just like she doesn't know the source of her anger—more than anger, vexation.

A darting thought crosses her mind, so quick she doesn't have time to catch and comprehend it. Something about primitive exchanges. Bartering as basic social interaction. Why not. There's something beautiful there. Something essential and human.

The house she stops at is very similar to hers. Unassuming, single-story, low windows. The main difference is that the yard is around back, not out front, and so she has to stand right in front of the door, which is ajar. She clears her throat and gives a timid knock. She realizes suddenly that she doesn't know the German's real name. She pokes her head inside, says anybody home, but it sounds more like a statement than a question. In fact, her voice doesn't even sound like her own; it rings false, like she's reading a part in a play. Anybody home, she repeats. There is no answer, and she steps inside. The house smells like damp wood and toast. There are only a few pieces of furniture, clothes hung on a foldable drying rack, and a television set, small and obsolete, on a shelf. From the tabletop, a tiger cat watches her, absolutely still. Nat walks past the cat, through the house, and exits out the back door leading to the garden. The German is squatting beside some furrows in the dirt. He turns and looks at her, unsurprised, as if her coming had only been a matter of time. He wipes his forehead on his arm.

"You came."

He comes over to her, hesitant. Nat observes him: muddy, glasses askance, sweating, ungainly, and recalls what he said days prior—it's been a long time since I was with a woman—and she understands, right then and there, how crucial that sentence is to his proposal in her mind, the dimension Nat herself invests in those words. What is she about to do? Have charity sex?

"Did you change your mind?" he asks. "The rain make you change your mind?"

Nat nods.

"You want it now? Here?"

Instinctively, she nods again. Suddenly, the question seems impertinent, almost absurd, but he's already dropping his tools, brushing off his hands.

"Give me a few minutes. I'm going to shower."

He smiles at her as he walks inside: a tight smile, abashed perhaps, but also bright and quick. She remains outside, looking at the garden. Another pair of skittish cats, skinnier than one inside, pass by on their way to the shed at the back, where his sacks, firewood, and tools are stored. The dirt gives off a strong odor of manure, or trash. Nat observes the sky, the clouds crowding in the distance. The smell, the wind on her skin, the mix of green and brown hues—leaves and dirt—the bitter taste of her saliva—nerves—all that anchors her in that moment is expressed through her senses, and yet, she is overwhelmed with a sense of unreality, the conceptual eclipsing the material, as if instead being on the edge of a new lived experience, she was an actor on set, participating in a great big farce. The German doesn't take long. He comes out for her with wet hair, combed back. He points at the rotting pepper plants.

"What's good for some plants destroys others."

She realizes he is just talking to decrease the tension. His commentary, however, only makes it worse. A sullen crease creeps to her lips. She needs it to be over fast. He seems to notice and so leads her inside, where, after gently taking her arm, he points to a darkened bedroom. His voice softens as he explains that it's better like this, in the dark. He doesn't want her to be uncomfortable, he says. He doesn't want her to feel upset or offended, he repeats.

"We'll finish quick."

As her eyes adjust to the dark, Nat sees a small, unmade bed. He asks her to lie down, please, on her back. She can take off all her clothes or only the necessary articles, whatever she prefers. Nat lies on the bed and strips from the waist down. The German looks away, as if he'd rather not watch. The sheets are slightly damp but clean, as if he'd put them on before they were completely dry. Still turned away from her, he explains what they will do. Nat finds a sort of professional detachment—not indifference—in his words, as though he meant to remind her that their encounter constituted a commercial transaction. And yet beneath the tone there's a tremble of uncertainty, a failure to entirely contain his unease. In that moment, Nat feels a tenuous tenderness, something ephemeral that disappears in a flash. She thinks: here is a man I would never be attracted to. This is how it has to be, like this, in the gloom: a man who attempts to conceal his jitters as he takes off his shirt and pants; a woman who waits, prepared to surrender, not knowing, really, what purpose that surrender serves.

That's how she sees it then: as a surrender, a handing over. Something she cedes to him in exchange for something else.

Everything unfolds according to his plan. He is already very aroused when he climbs on top of her. First on his knees, gauging the space between her legs, his head bent, not meeting her eyes. Nat sees the shape of his penis; observes it with curiosity as he opens a condom and carefully rolls it on. He slides closer. She opens herself, lifts her hips to aid his access. She lets him enter. She lets him be inside. That was his request: to be inside, a little while. Smooth and slow, she feels his hardness along her insides, the chafing in spite of his efforts to be gentle. She closes her eyes. The German has held himself up so as not to crush her, hands firmly placed on either side of her body, but then allows himself to drop, runs his hands along her sides, taking his time, until he reaches the hem of her T-shirt—where her flesh begins—at her naked waist—and stops. Nat hears a soft grunt, feels the jolt of release, and lets him stay inside a little longer, as his body relaxes. The rain has picked up again, plinking rhythmically on the sheet metal roof of the shed out back. A cat meows pitifully, and the German pulls out, gets dressed, and leaves so she can clean herself up and put on her clothes in peace.

When she comes out of the room, they don't talk about what has happened. Maybe, she thinks, silence is part of the deal. She's not sure if it has been what he expected or not. So long since he'd been with a woman, he'd said, and now he has been with her. Did she meet his expectations? Despite the brief nature of the encounter, despite the distance between them, did he obtain the pleasure he sought? Brevity and distance, those were the conditions he had imposed. Maybe he thought it would be less upsetting for her, or maybe his ground rules were a personal preference, a choice.

She is hit with a sudden, irrepressible need to know his name. Once, she heard him called Andrea, but she doubts that's it because Andrea is a woman's name. Maybe it's Andreas, with an s. An s that here in La Escapa, no one's ever going to pronounce. Her understanding is that Andreas is a Greek name, but maybe it's also used in Germany. Is that why they all just make things easy and call him the German? Nat won't ask. If she knows anything, it's that those kinds of questions make no sense in the context of what's just happened between them. She pets the tiger cat—a female, it turns out— while the German—Andreas, or whatever his name is—looks for an umbrella to lend her. The rain is worsening, but it goes without saying that she doesn't want to hang around. Or is he the one who's reluctant to have her stay?

He doesn't thank her when they say goodbye. As it should be, Nat thinks, this wasn't an act of charity or altruism. Still, her chest feels tight and she wants something more. A small show of gratitude, perhaps; sure, that would be nice.

That night she can hardly sleep, bombarded by her own doubts. Did she behave like a whore? How is she supposed to interpret what happened? How would a third party define it? If, at the time, she'd received money, cash money, if, for instance, he had left it on the bedside table, would it have a different meaning? It would for her, since she doesn't want any money—she just wants him to fix the problem of the roof, which is, ultimately, the problem of the landlord. But would the transaction not be the same if he'd given her money and, with that money, she hired a mason? Isn't it the same result? No, she concludes. Such a scenario would have simply introduced more links in the chain—the money, the mason—elements that did not form part of their pact.

Eliminating money, money that can be seen and touched, allows her to finally determine that she hadn't prostituted herself. But her apprehension persists. Isn't she looking for a way to justify herself, to make clean that which clearly is not? Does she really believe that getting a few leaks fixed should have to come to that? Or had she waited for the rain in order to have an excuse? Had there been no other way to get the money? If she'd had enough for Sieso's shots and vet visits, why wouldn't she have the money for repairs? Or, if the landlord refused to fix the roof, she could have threatened to move out. She could have left. She has no ties to La Escapa. There are plenty of similar places around those parts: oak groves, cropland, dirt roads. There's no shortage of cheap houses—including ones without leaky roofs.

She tries to consider the situation from an outside point of view. To see herself through the others' eyes, watching and judging her. No one would buy her reasoning. Why should they? They would say she did it because, deep down, it was what she wanted. That she liked it. That when it comes to sex, there is no gray area between pleasure and disgust: and if she hadn't felt disgust, well, then it was clear what she *had* felt. Would it have been more dignified on her part if she'd been repulsed, if she'd felt upset or hurt, humiliated or used? If the encounter had lasted longer? Or if he had obliged her to move, suck, bite, writhe?

But the whole act had lasted only a few minutes. So many questions cannot fit in so little time. Maybe, she tells herself, she must deal with it more simply: the German made an offer; at first, she didn't think it was appropriate, but later, she did. She isn't required to define the act with any specific term. He was sincere and clean. No hemming and hawing, no obnoxious advances like those of her neighbor. The German expressed his needs, made his request, offered something in return—something she really needs. The encounter was as matter-of-fact as it had to be, not sordid or denigrating. She tries to remember it step by step, move by move. What did he say, which words did he use, at which exact moment? Repulsion or regret—what she might've feared—hadn't materialized. The German had shown sensitivity. A delicacy she, admittedly, hadn't imagined in him, with his coarse and not exactly sophisticated appearance. He had tried not to hurt her, bearing his weight on his hands, going slow. She still feels the heat between her legs, heat considerably more mental than physical. Even though it was quick, the sensation that prevails is one of slowness. How can she explain it?

Now she must avoid misunderstandings at all costs. He must not think there will be other opportunities, because there won't. If a misunderstanding should arise, she will be firm. Nip it in the bud. The potential appeal of what happened between them—she later decides that the word *appeal* is an imprudent word, and replaces it with *incentive*—the potential incentive, she thinks, resides in the one-off nature of the proposal. Even if he were to suggest another encounter, under the same terms, the circumstances would be wildly different: the body has memory, and to repeat is to reinforce it. That's the last thing she wants.

The next morning, the German arrives in his van and gets to work. Nat offers him coffee. No, thanks, he already had one. While he evaluates the damage to the tiles outside, she sits down at her computer.

"Here if you need me," she says.

She realizes the words are ambiguous and is embarrassed. Nothing she can say is innocent now. This conclusion is irritating. Not a consequence she would have considered beforehand.

It's impossible to concentrate with him outside, so close. A single sentence, even the simplest ones, takes her ages to translate. In fact, the simplest sentences resist the most. The temptation to quit surfaces again. Why persist in doing something she's clearly bad at? Once or twice she gets up to look at herself in the mirror: baggy-eyed and pale. Not her best day. She brushes her hair, puts on a little make-up. She returns to her seat. She perseveres, brooding at length over the same paragraph.

The German pokes his head inside, startling her. He says he's going to Petacas to get the new roof tiles. He'll have some work to do inside, too, when he gets back; he hopes it won't bother her, he'll try to finish fast. Okay, Nat says, and a shiver runs through her when he leaves. Won't bother, will finish fast: the same expressions he used the day before, spoken, even, with the same pronunciation, that incoherent crowding of syllables. Doesn't he know how to talk any other way?

The repair takes the whole day. The German waterproofs the surface, both outside and inside the house, and lays the new tiles. He'll install a gutter, too, he explains, to channel the runoff and keep the water from pooling on the roof. Nat doesn't tally up the cost of the tiles, the gutter, and the waterproof paint, plus the few other products he has bought, the purpose of which she is ignorant. All of that, plus the labor hours, the required knowledge and skill, is the price he put on her body yesterday afternoon. Is it a lot, is it a little? He's said nothing about it. He's said the bare minimum. He only breaks for a smoke, wandering around the property in complete silence. Nat thinks: he wants to leave me alone, he thinks otherwise I might be uncomfortable. But it's his reserve that really makes her uncomfortable. So cold, she thinks. And simultaneously: What did she expect? Warmth? It would be worse, so much worse, if he were to do the opposite, if he were to be affectionate or even suggestive; if he were to remind her that he's had access to her innermost self and that such a step cannot be untaken.

The hours pass and her anger grows. She can't translate, she can't read, she can't focus. Even Sieso's presence is annoying.

When she sees the German is finally picking up his things, she thinks about offering him a beer, but he just leans inside to say goodbye—he doesn't come in, doesn't even cross the threshold—and she drops it. He probably has better things to do, she thinks. His garden, for example. Or some other odd job, a repair like the one he's just done for her, who knows. She sees him off with detachment, only thanking him at the last minute. Another mistake, she thinks: it isn't she who should be thanking him, but the other way around.

"I saw the German fiddling around on your roof," Píter says.

He says fiddling around with subtle contempt, and Nat, feeling caught out, overexplains. He fixed a little problem with some leaks, she says. He didn't charge much and he did a good job, too, clean and quick—she blushes: clean and quick. Wait, she had to pay him? Really? Píter is scandalized. No, no, of course not, the landlord will take care of it. Eyebrow raised—his habitual expression—Píter declares that the German does sloppy work. He doesn't understand why she called him when he—Píter—could have helped. A few leaks are easy enough to fix.

"I think he did a good job," Nat insists. "He spent the whole day. He put in a lot of time."

"That doesn't mean anything. Putting in a lot of time is not synonymous with dedication. It can also signal clumsiness. Or chutzpah: just so he can justify his bill. What did he charge?"

Nat stammers.

"I told you, I didn't pay."

"But you don't even know what he's going to charge?"

"I have no idea, he struck a deal with the landlord."

"You said he was cheap before."

"Well, that's what I inferred. The landlord is such a tight-wad, it couldn't have been much."

"The German and the landlord striking a deal!" Píter clucks his tongue. "I don't know how you can trust them."

Nat laughs, admits her mistake, but what can she do about it now? she says. She doesn't know if the German is a sloppy worker, but he is an odd duck, that's for sure. Why do they call him the German? Isn't his name Andreas or something? Andreas, yeah, Píter confirms. His mother was German, or Kurdish, or a Kurd living in Germany, he can't remember. Was he born there, in Germany? No, Píter doesn't think so, he doesn't know. He came to La Escapa about five years ago, he's never talked about his past. He's always on his own, does whatever jobs come his way and, yes, Píter repeats, he's sloppy. As far as he knows, the German has worked as a framer in Petacas, and as a deliveryman, too. He fixes plumbing, does odd jobs, stuff like that. Now he works in his garden. Gets by on small things. But he doesn't talk to anyone, doesn't have friends. Píter doesn't buy the excuse that he's reserved. In a place as small as La Escapa, such isolation is suspicious. That's why he says the German can't be trusted. Among other reasons.

"What reasons?"

"Reasons. I don't know, stuff he does or I heard he does."

"Stuff like . . . ?"

"Oh Nat, I don't remember right now."

"But if you don't remember, why did you just say it like that, like it was something really serious?"

Píter smiles, not a smile that inspires intimacy, but the opposite: the coolness of someone who knows more, or insinuates that he does.

"Hey, why the sudden interest? What do you care about the German? You're like, all defensive."

Nat smiles too. Just curious, she assures him. He spent the whole day at her house, after all. And yes, one has to admit, his silence is rather peculiar. He hardly talked.

She's awoken by the sound of rain. A fickle, offbeat pinging, the drops falling on the gutter bought and installed by the German, the gutter he promised would channel water to the ground in an orderly fashion, prevent it from accumulating between the tiles. This sound transports Nat back to his house, to the day when it rained on the shed's metal roof. The moment the rain started, he'd run his hands over her sides—the only caress she received—from her underarms to her hips, from the fabric of her shirt to her bare skin, slow and gentle. She is startled by the memory. She turns on the light and tries to read, but it's no use. A chill runs down her spine. She feels anxious, like an animal in heat. What's wrong with her?

She returns to her translation at daybreak. *Ce n'était pas une vision. J'ai touché ses cheveux . . .* The words ring in her head: hollow, mute, shapeless, until they begin to take on meaning, all possible meanings. Touch the mane or stroke the mane?

Touch sounds bad, but it's what appears in the original text. If it was referring to stroking, wouldn't the author have written *caresser*? And mane? Why not *hair*? After all, isn't it more natural to stroke the hair, touch the hair? How would she say it? Touch the waist or stroke the waist? What's the difference between touching and stroking? She translates: *It wasn't a vision. I touched her mane.* Rereading it, her revulsion builds. She stands and walks around the room. Sieso watches her, but the dog's gaze is not clear: there is judgment behind his eyes.

A couple of hours later, someone calls from outside, clearly pronouncing her name. The German is on the other side of the gate: patient, resolute, calm, in his work clothes and ill-fitting glasses. He's just coming to check that things are okay. With last night's rain, he repeats, was it okay? So that's it, Nat thinks. That's all? He's here to ask about the work? She replies drily.

"Good, thanks. Tight as a drum."

He breaks into a crooked smile: satisfaction for a job well done. That's what brought him here? Nat thinks. Nothing else? Really, nothing else? He doesn't think he owes her an apology, an explanation, a sign of gratitude at least? Great, he says, just what I wanted to hear.

"If you have any trouble, let me know," he adds before turning back towards the road.

Nat freezes. Infuriated. She doesn't want him to go, and yet she needs him to leave immediately. She detests his tone, the absolute lack of tact in his choice of words. If you have any trouble, he said. And what about the other trouble? She hasn't felt so bad, so wretched, in a long time.

What's he after, turning up at her house without warning? What right does he have? Everybody in these small villages does it, sure, but what a rude custom! She was relaxing—or trying to relax—she didn't want to see anybody, she certainly didn't want to see him. But suddenly he appeared and she—hair unwashed, face unwashed, in her pajamas—had to act like it was all perfectly normal, swallow her pride, ape a cordial and neighborly coexistence after they'd made a simple transaction—sex in exchange for roof repair? Insane. The concern, the respect, how's it going, everything okay with the rain, if you have any trouble, let me know. He can't even tell I'm angry, Nat thinks. Not even. Two days ago he had her in his room and he's just looked at her with complete disinterest, like he would look at a goat or a dog. Maybe he even regrets what he did to her, seeing her now, in the light of day. So long without a woman and all he got was her, that mess.

She runs into Joaquín and Roberta on her way to the shop. The old couple pick their way down the muddy roadside, arm in arm. Nat catches up to them quickly. They're not going anywhere in particular; just out for a stroll. Joaquín says they need to stretch their legs. The doctor has recommended they walk: it's good for their health, physical, and mental too. He winks complicitly. Roberta shows signs of recognizing Nat, smiles at her warmly and says a polite hello. But Nat senses that the old woman can't quite place her; for a moment, she confuses her with the shopgirl, then with somebody named Sofía, who must be a relative. She speaks courteously, neatly, with accurate vocabulary and complex verbal structures, but what she says doesn't make any sense: there's an enormous gap between the logic of her language and that of reality. Joaquín arches his eyebrows expressively, as if apologizing. Then Roberta asks about the dog.

"The dog?"

"Yes, the skinny dog. Is he better?"

Nat is happy the conversation is heading toward safe terrain.

"I brought him to the vet. He got his shots and he's eating good food now. I think he's even put on a little weight. But he still doesn't trust me. It's possible he was abused."

"With the bricks."

"With the bricks? I don't know what they used . . . rocks, or . . . who knows what."

Roberta's eyes, ink-dark and clear, lock on Nat's.

"No! Not the dog! The German and the bricks."

The German. She can't have misheard. The old woman has distinctly said his name.

"What's happening with the bricks?" Joaquín says.

"Everything!"

Now she speaks in frustration, wanting to be understood. She points a finger at Nat.

"She gives him the fruit and he lays the bricks."

Nat is dumbstruck, mouth agape. The old man perseveres.

"The fruit? The fruit isn't the girl's. It's the German's. From his garden. He sells it. We buy it from him, too. Remember?"

Roberta laughs softly, as if recalling something amusing. Muttering to herself, head bent, she repeats: *she gives him the fruit and he lays the bricks*. Nat tries to understand. Maybe the old woman saw Andreas going up on the roof, just like Píter saw him, just like other people in La Escapa will have done. Maybe by *bricks* she means tiles. But what does she mean about the fruit? The vegetables from the garden? Or something else? She shakes her head.

She must not assign any importance to the words of a crazy old woman. It's Nat herself, Nat and her own susceptibleness, that prompts her to see everything from the wrong angle.

She shows up at night. Not on impulse this time. She's thought it through and taken the time to get ready: to shave, shower, wash her hair, blow it dry, put on perfume, choose clothes she thinks are flattering. Part of her is conscious of the contradiction in her preparations. If all she wants is to talk—sort things out, clarify the situation, whatever—all the grooming is unnecessary. But the two things aren't mutually exclusive, she later thinks, as if defending herself before an impassive judge. She's nervous when she leaves the house, her chest tight. She takes the car because night has fallen and, for the moment, the neighbors' petitions for better lighting have not borne fruit. She drives slowly, trying not to make noise; her plan consists of suddenly appearing on his doorstep, unannounced, getting her revenge. The silence, however, is absolute—denser, deeper than ever—and everything she does upon her arrival—park, turn off the engine, pull the handbrake—reverberates counter to her intentions. Stepping with care on the pebbled drive, she reaches the house and knocks; there's no doorbell, at least not one she can find. She hears the TV volume being lowered inside and then footsteps approaching. The German opens the door, looks at her in surprise, asks her to come in. At the sight of him, Nat feels a jolt of fury and resentment—that obstinate, slow look on his face, as if he was clueless about what was happening—and wonders if she's making another mistake. Her voice is unnatural when she asks if she can talk to him for a few minutes. Sure, of course, he replies, and mutes—but doesn't turn off—the TV. He clears a spot on the couch for her to sit—moves pillows, shoos off the tiger cat—and asks her if she wants a beer, which she declines. He sits down in an ugly, frayed old armchair across from her. She does have time to notice that: the chair is ugly and frayed.

But they won't talk. Not then, not in the coming hours, not the whole night.

From that day on, the stream of her thoughts is completely redirected. Thoughts no longer flow where they used to. Now they go wherever they want, toward other places, and they cannot be dammed.

It's like a film is playing in her mind. Parading images of Andreas, her and Andreas, Andreas and her, in bed. His body, her body, every movement, the wrinkled sheets, every one of the—few—words they said to each other. The movie ends too soon, it is despairingly short, she rewatches it again and again, idles in the details, extends each shot so it lasts, includes prior scenes—her arrival at his house—and subsequent ones—their goodbyes, her leaving—although these last ones leave a bitter, murky taste in her mouth. Still, it isn't much. Far from enough. Nat doesn't exactly know *why* she wants to prolong the reel. It is a need she hasn't bothered to understand. She simply carries it with her, carries it everywhere, unable to disconnect from the images now imprinted on her, in her, now projected through her eyes, everywhere she looks, anywhere at all.

Is it an obsession? Yes, it is clearly an obsession. But not only that, she thinks. It's a rapture, a metamorphosis, a radical transformation of the predictable. What was once outside, far off on the horizon, what was invisible and uninteresting, is now inside of her, inhabiting her, wracking her.

Hierarchies have changed. Everything is in disarray.

In order to explain it to herself, she must invoke something foreign, an external force. The first day, the day they sealed their strange pact, Andreas injected his poison into her, that's what happened. Nat was ignorant of his ploy, but when she dressed and left his house, she was carrying it already, and the poison proceeded to spread through her veins, flooding her to devastating effect. From that first day on, stripped of her will, she had no choice but to return: poison demands more poison, there is no antidote. She didn't choose Andreas, she didn't seek him out: he inflicted himself on her. She should resist, but to struggle is futile: she is snared. That's how she sees him now.

It's her interpretation, a childish, magical interpretation—she is entirely aware of its flimsiness—but tremendously useful for justifying the way she yields.

Why resist? she asks herself. What does she gain? What is she going to lose?

She decides to go back again. And again. And again. The film reel grows, gets longer. It is never enough.

He is always willing to receive her. It's no longer a cold-blooded agreement, something that can be wrapped up in five minutes. Now, they spend hours and hours together, they catnap, they start again. They only stop to regather strength, unless the time comes for her to leave, and even then, there is no ending, there is never an end. Nat has never known anything like it, not like this. That man, Andreas, elicits something completely new from her, something insatiable and addictive. Aren't men supposed to slow down after a certain age? Andreas is tireless.

But he is not as voracious as Nat, or not as voracious as she would've imagined, given the circumstances. He doesn't demonstrate the exigency or tortured carnality she has experienced with other men—no dark side behind bedroom doors. Nor the desire to prevail, to win that war, subtle and undeclared, and akin, occasionally, to impotence. Andreas's sexuality is that of a simple man, she thinks, a placid man. The path they walk together involves no anguish, fear, or obscenity, no misgiving or insult. Naked, lying side by side, they are like siblings. Nat doesn't have to chase her orgasm, or claw desperately at its borders, begging to enter its domain. All she has to do is follow her body's signals, precise and pleasurable instructions that lead her to certain success. Her body has instinctively gained such wisdom that it hardly matters that he's a stranger. Are they joined by some secret knowledge, sacred and inaccessible to others? If so, it's a religious connection, like that which binds members of a cult to the exclusion of outsiders: the uninitiated, the neophyte, the ignorant.

And yet, when they are done, they cannot meet one another's eye and shame and small expressions of mistrust soon appear. Nat watches him in secret, fascinated by the body that has been hers and is now, suddenly, foreign again. Her own body also assumes another shape—an opposite form—as if the mirage of her agility, her beauty, dissolved, inhibited, in the void. When she pours a glass of water in the kitchen, her back to him, or when they sit across from each other under the citrine glow of the old ceiling lamp, their bodies are no longer allies, but adversaries again.

All it takes is a single touch, a new rapprochement, for the wheel to resume its spinning. Pique and desire, craving and vertigo: those are the alternating cogs.

Nat, the distant, impassible, aloof Nat, has been transformed into a ravenous creature. To such a degree that she must stop herself from going to him at all hours, from falling asleep there at night. He's never asked her to stay and she convinces herself it is for the best: preserve the spell of the illicit, see each other inconsistently, clandestinely. Even so, a part of her would love for Andreas to at least try to convince her to stay longer; there is always residual disappointment when she feels his eyes watching the road as she walks away. He never tries to change her mind.

Sex? Is it a matter of sex? If she concentrates on what's beneath her skin, the tyrannical and insistent quiver, then everything points to yes. Nevertheless, she refuses to reduce it to that. Sex has always been secondary to her. Pleasurable, sure—at times—but also pleasurably secondary: she could do without it no problem, she could forget it, even erase it from her life. Curiosity and coolness: that's how it's always been with her. The men that interested her were very different from Andreas. In general, she liked to listen to their stories—or take walks, see a movie, get drunk and laugh—much more than sleeping with them. She tired of all those activities eventually, but she always tired of sleeping with them first. Her body would close up at their touch, unbidden and disobedient. Frigid, she'd once been called, an accusation that seemed directed her whole personhood, not just her body.

When she was a kid, a man, a neighbor, had molested her. After those encounters, which occurred on several occasions, Nat had mostly felt confused—a bit of guilt, a bit of fear, but confusion, mostly—even though, as soon as she got rid of him, she'd gone on with life as if nothing had happened. The man would sit her on his lap, rub himself against her. He didn't hurt her. He was a good man, a man Nat's parents were very fond of, an old man—Nat remembers him as old, though he probably wasn't much older than fifty—solitary, a music lover with small, kindly eyes whose wife had died of cancer several years before. Nat couldn't speak badly of him to her parents, she didn't feel she had the right. And even though she started to avoid him, she was fond of him, too, in her own way. Had all of that conditioned her developing sexuality? Nat doesn't think so, despite what it said regarding cases like hers, all that stuff about the indelible marks from childhood. But even if it were true, even if the neighbor *had* turned her into a detached, insensitive person, now that has all changed, unexpectedly, thanks to another man.

Píter has been calling her nonstop. Nat says she's busy at first, then that she doesn't feel well, she has a terrible headache, her neck and back hurt too, it isn't good for her to be sitting for so long, translating. Her excuses are clumsy and rude, she knows, but she will explain everything to him later. The days go by, however, and she doesn't find a good time. Until one evening, when she is just about to leave the house, Píter appears at her door.

"You're a sight for sore eyes!" he says.

He looks her over, smiling but scowling, as if trying to solve a riddle. Does she have time for a beer? he asks. He's on his way to Petacas to get some shopping done. She could come along and they could get a drink, how does that sound?

Nat doesn't answer right away. Suddenly, an offer so simple, so ordinary, is hard for her to deal with. She shakes her head.

Another time. Another time? he laughs. He's come by a few times now and she's never in. What's she got to do that's so important? She's dressed and everything, he says, she just has to grab her purse. She doesn't even need to bring any money. His treat. Or is she on her way elsewhere?

"I was just going for a walk."

"Take a walk with me!"

"No, seriously, another time. I need some time on my own."

He raises his hands in a sign of peace. Cool, he says, he doesn't want to bother her. That's never been his intention. He thought she could use the company, especially if she's spent the previous days lonely and in pain, as she says. Or maybe she's had other company? Maybe she hasn't been that lonely.

"You don't have to hide anything from me."

Unease wends through her. Píter's voice contains no hint of reproach; the opposite, really, he's being sympathetic and kind, playful during a situation in which it's normal for friends to rib each other. But below it is the sense of moral obligation: Nat shouldn't lie to someone who has been so good to her. She says she's sorry. She admits she owes him an explanation. She promises she'll explain later, as soon as she can. Píter puts out a conciliatory hand. It's okay, he says, reaching out to rub her arm. Unconsciously, Nat recoils.

"I really have to go. I'll tell you everything soon, I promise."

"The details, anyway."

"What's that?"

"I mean, you'll tell me the details. I already know the basics."

"Of what?"

"You and the German."

Nat goes blank as Píter smiles sardonically. The basics? Does he mean her visits to Andreas—her frequent and private visits—which he must have heard about? Or the rest of it, too—their agreement over the roof?

From a few meters away, Sieso observes the scene, hieratic, ears pricked, his eyes slits. Anubis, she thinks fuzzily: maybe she should call him Anubis, the embalmers' jackal, a god of strange physiognomy, but a god nonetheless. Píter shakes her from her trance. Solemnity has returned to his full and mild face. He strokes his beard as he speaks, as if in reflection, underscoring the weight of his words.

"Honey, this is La Escapa. A handful of houses in the middle of nowhere. What did you expect? That no one would find out? I just want you to be okay."

"I am okay."

"That's all I want. If you're okay, then I have no opinion. Forget what I said last time."

"What do you mean?"

"Last time, when you asked about him and I told you that I didn't trust him. You were trying to get me to talk, weren't you?"

She blushes, but Píter hurries to clarify—again—that he isn't upset, he completely understands and has no objections, *just as long as she's okay.*

What is it with all this insistence? Are his words a warning? When Nat says goodbye, it's with only slight concern, hardly significant because, at the moment, her urgency to leave—her desire—outweighs it.

But those ounces of suspicion will later start to multiply, to take on heft.

"Did you like me from the beginning?"

No, Andreas says. There's no hesitation. He doesn't even pretend to think about it: a categorial and impassive *no*. Actually, he adds, he hardly noticed her. He saw her out on the roads, or in the shop, but she didn't pique his interest. He doesn't pay much attention. It always happens to him, with everyone. Nat feels a pain in her throat. Bitter and sharp, well-aimed. Inexplicable. She has trouble swallowing.

"So, I could have been anybody."

It's only mid-afternoon, but the light in the bedroom is murky, as if it were already dusk. They can barely make out the other's face. Andreas deliberates a few seconds and then looks up at the ceiling.

"You could be someone else and so could I. That's the way it always is."

"But if I hadn't come looking for you after . . . the first time, none of this would have happened?"

"Maybe not."

"Wow, it really hurts to hear you say that."

He smiles absently.

"It shouldn't. In the end, it did happen. You are you and I am me. That's what matters."

Nat would like to ask what she means to him. She would like to say that, if everything started by chance—chance as petty, as trivial, as a leaky roof—then she doesn't understand why they keep seeing each other, since their agreement has been satisfied. She knows it's ridiculous but, deep down, she would like to be his chosen woman, to have been seduced following careful plotting. She would like to hear that Andreas noticed her on day one, slowly fell in love, over time, concocted plans to get close to her, saw his opportunity and took it, ignoring the risk: a romantic narrative to replace the . . . pornographic? But Andreas says none of this. He just observes her solemnly, as if her pain was contrived and he should be charitable and overlook it, at most.

"Well, did you notice me?" he asks at last. "Isn't it the same thing?"

Nat turns toward the wall to hide her tears. It all started in that very bed, she thinks, when he told her to strip from the waist down if that's what she preferred. He used her because the prostitutes in Petacas were, he said, awful. How should he know? Had he resorted to them on other occasions? Tired of the whores' wretchedness, he decided it was better to approach her? What kind of person does that?

Andreas moves closer, rubs her back, kisses the curve of her neck. Can't she be content with the facts? he says. The facts on their own? Why does she need to interpret everything? What does she hope to achieve? Nat doesn't respond. Lying on her side, arms crossed, she tries to expel the devil taking her over.

She wakes on Saturday to the sound of her neighbors' voices in their yard. They must have arrived the previous evening and now are frenetic with party preparations. Nat hears them talk about pork chops, charcoal, lighter cubes. The children fight over a toy in high-pitched, exasperating little voices. Nat puts a pillow over her head. It was very late when she got home from Andreas's—she'd waited until the last minute for him to ask her to spend the night, waited to refuse the invitation—and now the ruckus will prevent her from sleeping in. She gets out of bed but makes no move to do anything in particular. Her translation is still on the table where she left it, a page containing a reflection on silence, *de notre silence en particulier, une qualité de silence en particulier.* But if silence is the absence of words, how can there be a silence *in particular?* Shouldn't all silences be the same, like the color white is always the same? So, what differentiates silences are their surroundings, obviously—starting with the cause. Andreas's silence at the end of sex, is it the same as hers? Nat senses it is not, that it is made of other stuff.

She hears Sieso's bark and goes out on the porch. Píter is by the gate. His magnificent dog wags her tail beside him, drooling with excitement. Nat and Píter haven't mentioned Andreas again. They, too, have chosen a kind of particular silence. She promised to give him more details, but when she thinks about it, what sort of details can she provide? The details are gratuitous. They could even be counterproductive.

"I'm taking these over to the Cottage," he says, holding up a case of beer. "See you over there."

"Over there? What do you mean?"

"The autumn party, the party to celebrate the . . ."

93

He sets the beer down, pensive. That's weird, he mutters, rubbing his temple. They didn't invite you? Every year, her neighbors throw a party to welcome the season. It's a La Escapa tradition, he explains. They must have just forgot.

"Want me to remind them?"

Nat vehemently shakes her head.

"What do I care about their party? I don't belong there."

But Píter looks displeased. He insists on mediating. It's important for everyone in the community to get along. On the word *community*, his eyebrows arch in seriousness.

"Well, I'm sure I'm not the only person they didn't invite. I'm sure they didn't invite the gypsies. Or Roberta. It's not like they're obligated to invite everyone, are they?"

"Oh, come on," Píter protests. "You know that's not the same."

"Yes, it is. And it would be worse if it weren't. Even less reason to go."

Nat, truthfully, doesn't care about her neighbors. She feels contempt when she sees them acting like the Cottage is actually a beautiful home on a beautiful estate, she derides the invisible pressure they put on themselves—and their children—to look happy all the time. And yet, a part of her—an amphibian, or reptilian, part—is intrigued by the fact that they have excluded her. Why? How has she offended them?

But she feigns indifference in front of Píter and later, too, when telling Andreas about it in a fit of uncontrolled loquacity. She isn't upset, she claims, although she is surprised to be excluded like that. They probably reject her way of life. They must not approve of her living there alone, of the fact that she doesn't have a husband to mow the lawn, that she's over thirty and has no kids—and no plans to have them—that she doesn't worry about La Escapa's sewers or the strength of the local school system, topics heavily debated by so many of their friends the last time. They've almost certainly found out about Andreas, about their—she hesitates, looking for the right word—friendship. They must find that condemnable, as well.

"Couldn't it be that they simply forgot you?" Andreas interrupts.

Nat senses she's being accused of something, though she's unsure of what. Being a drama queen? A victim? Self-centered? No, they didn't forget, she says. That's impossible. They live right next door, their properties abut. And they've invited her before. No, she just has to accept that they don't like her.

"But you don't like them either, right?"

"Of course not."

"Would you invite them over?"

"I wouldn't even have a barbecue."

Andreas smiles.

"Then what do you care? You're speaking different languages."

By now, the whole of La Escapa knows the situation between her and Andreas. Like Píter warned her, in such a small place, in such a limited community, it would be naïve to think they hadn't all been talking about her for days. She notices how the girl acts differently when she goes to the shop, cooler, distant, as if she'd been slighted. Her mother, who used to come out of the back to say hello, clearly avoids Nat, pretending to be busy in the storeroom. In Gordo's bar, she has to deal with the glances and whispers of the construction crews from Petacas, appraising her on the sly. Nat is disheartened. Why does every-thing have to be so hostile, so complicated? Even her landlord seems to know something, or she imagines that he does. The day he turns up to collect the rent, knocking ostentatiously on the front door, he points snidely to the gutter.

"Whoever did that really knew what he was doing."

A thought crosses Nat's mind, like a shadow. Maybe the landlord knows about more than her relationship with An-dreas, maybe he knows the terms on which it was established, the chain of causes and consequences that, if put into words, would sound forced and even preposterous. But the landlord doesn't say more. Nothing about the possibility of discounting her rent to cover the repair. No word of thanks, either. He sim-ply takes the envelope and asks about Sieso. How's the beast? he says. The *beast*. It's a word that, as of late, Nat has encoun-tered often while translating. *Bête*, though here its meaning is different. Disrespectful.

"He's great."

"Yeah? Guess I have to take your word for it. I never see him."

"That's because he hides."

The landlord guffaws.

"Hides? So he hides now, does he? And who does he hide from? Me? That's rich!"

"I didn't say from whom. I just said that he hides. He's a solitary dog. Does his own thing."

Does his own thing: a conclusive statement, proud, one that confers some dignity on the dog. It would be fairer, more appropriate, to say that Sieso is surly. Bad-tempered. But that would mean making a concession to the landlord, ceding in the struggle that is taking place between them on another level, behind their words.

"Is that why you tie him up at night, because he 'does his own thing'?"

Nat pales. How does he know that? Does he prowl around at night, too? She can't speak without her chin quivering. Like when, as a child, she was caught in a lie.

"I tie him up because I don't want him to fight with other dogs. They all go mad before the sun comes up, all of them barking at the same time."

"Mad? Girl, they're dogs! What do you want them to do? They're dogs, period. The worst thing you can do to a dog is tie him up. A dog needs to make his rounds. Fuck around, look for bitches. If you don't leave him loose, he really will go mad."

Fuck around, look for bitches. Is that what the landlord does when he hangs around La Escapa at night? Nat feels a pit in her stomach, her legs go weak. If only she had the power to order the man out that very instant.

Tamely, she waits for him to leave.

She makes a meticulous study of Andreas's behavior, his tone of voice, the way he sits close to her or leaves space between them on the couch. Like a person taking scrupulous inventory, she registers the number of times he touches her hand or looks at her—even fleetingly—or how he pays attention when she tells him something, scouring the inflection in his voice for amiability or impatience. It's never enough. When they nod off in bed, for example, she feels he pulls away too soon, or holds her too little, rolling over and falling immediately into a deep sleep that excludes her entirely. She watches him and thinks: How does he manage it? How can he forget her presence, right there beside him? Nat dozes off and on, for just a few minutes and out of pure exhaustion, only to startle awake, heart pounding, distressed to discover they are no longer touching, that each one is on his or her own side of the bed, no contact at all.

The same thing happens with food. Nat has a lump in her throat that makes swallowing difficult, even chewing is an effort. In contrast, she watches him eat, eat with gusto, putting her aside the instant his fork spears or knife cuts, focused only on his utensils and the plate in front of him. Nat wonders what goes through his mind then. Does he completely forget her, does his hunger cast her aside? The contrast is brutal: she can't detach from him for even a second.

She feels true rage sometimes. Her own personality has been evicted so that he can occupy her completely and she, submissively, has *let him enter*. But what about him? What has he given her in exchange? He seems impervious to everything, barely allows for contact. If she tells him something personal, he listens to her in silence, making no comment. He doesn't ask for specifics nor does he try to interpret the events. The courteous attitude, which she usually finds lacking in others, is frustrating coming from Andreas. Can she chalk it up to his character, so cautious and reserved? Maybe he doesn't want to seem to pry? Or is he simply not that interested? He doesn't talk much about himself, and when he does, it's only in reference to external things, insignificant subjects, far removed from the two of them. His anonymous and anodyne tone makes Nat feel strangely humiliated, as if she were chasing someone who wants nothing to do with her, jogging ridiculously behind a person who doesn't even know she's there.

Other times, however, she lets herself be carried away by the headiness of the moment and believes she will explode with happiness. Holding his hand, still dazed and recovering from pleasure, she feels as though a cyclone has knocked her down and dragged her off to another world. When Andreas gets up, she buries her face in the sheets, tracking the scent of his sweat, practically in tears, repeating his name in a whisper. She tells herself that there is no greater union between two people than what they have. Maybe he's right. Maybe it's better to not plumb the mystery, not try and understand it, not risk its ruin.

She is haunted now by the idea of happiness's ache: a kind of happiness that contains within it the seed of its own destruction.

She asks him one day what his cat is called. Li, he says. Li? Just Li? Yeah, *L-I*. The cat doesn't need a last name, does it?

"Why Li?" she persists. "Does it have any special meaning?"

"No, not at all."

"It's pretty," she murmurs, just to say something, dodging the sense of having made a mistake, though she can't imagine what she did wrong.

It's hard to get anywhere with Andreas. Whenever she asks him something, his answers smack of closure, a preemptive signal that to press is futile. Maybe the odd thing about the way he talks is not, as Nat thought, the crowding of syllables, but the unequivocal tone, so self-sufficient, that underlies his speech.

Furtively, she watches him as he lies on his back, his eyes closed, at rest. When he finally falls asleep, she props herself up on her elbow so she can study him more closely, greedily. She looks for the traces of previous generations in his features—the Turkish, the German—the ones she doesn't know about because he never discusses his past. She reads his face and in it she finds a distinct majesty: his face is exactly as it should be, she thinks. Taken separately, the individual features lack beauty; they are, in fact, even common: the hooked nose, the lips tucked under the coarse, graying mustache, the violet shadows that render his eye sockets even more pronounced. And yet, she is captivated by the combination as a whole.

One must see him like this, like she does, to appreciate that face which is beyond the reach of others. Decisive, hard, full of secrets. It is a disconcerting face.

Impossible to access what lie behind his eyelids.

Lately, Andreas has been neglecting his garden. Even Nat, who knows nothing about plants, can see that. Maybe he hasn't needed to water, not with all the rain, but one can't simply rely on the weather: a good portion of the vegetables are getting spoiled precisely because of the excess water. Plants sitting in puddles, rotting sprouts, branches gone wild, twisting out of control, dirt dug up by the cats that come in to steal Li's food . . . this is her view of the garden now. Since they've been together, Andreas only picks vegetables for his own consumption. He no longer distributes produce to the neighbors, at least not to her knowledge. When she asks, he waves his hand, an unconcerned, or maybe apathetic, gesture. The garden isn't important, he says. I was planning on quitting it sooner or later.

"Well, it would be a shame. Everything you grow is great."

Andreas nods. Yeah, it is. Or was. But the time has come to do something else.

Something else? At first, Nat believes he is referring to her—to the time he spends with her—but her intuition veers quickly in another direction. She is on alert.

As he rolls a cigarette, Andreas explains that last year, a friend of his—an acquaintance, really—set up a land surveyance company in Petacas. At first he just ran it by himself, but he's already put together a modest portfolio of clients and needs more people. So he's going to work with him, as a topographer. He's actually going to start next week, in just a few days. He doesn't have high expectations but, no matter how small the village, the town administrators all brag about their urban development projects and public works. Basically, it will be that kind of work: a steady drip of small jobs.

Nat has been listening to him, mouth agape, surprised to hear terms she never would have imagined him saying, expressions like *modest portfolio of clients* and *urban development projects*. Wasn't Andreas just a guy from the country? Now, suddenly, one must presume that he is educated, has a degree, culture, all things she had never expected. A flurry of doubts arise within her, questions she wants to ask piling up behind her teeth. What, exactly, do topographers do? Measure terrain? Draw maps? What kinds of instruments do they use? Tape, levels, compasses, GPS? Who do they work with? Public works, construction companies, businesspeople? She simply can't imagine Andreas handling official documentation or writing reports. The mere possibility of him using a computer strikes her as exceedingly strange. He doesn't have one at home and even his cellphone is shockingly rudimentary.

She blurts out a question, unexpectedly violent.

"But did you—*you*—go to school for that?"

Andreas looks up, observes her seriously. A wrinkle marks his forehead when he replies.

Of course, he says. He studied Geography in Cárdenas, longer ago than she would believe. Is she surprised? What does she think a topographer should look like? Did she really think he was only good for planting lettuce? He laughs, but his laugh comes from a distance, from a place she has been banished from. Nat apologizes and goes outside. She squats down and pokes in the dirt, doubtful. Píter didn't tell her any of this. He had shown disdain, saying simply that Andreas was a sloppy worker. Did Píter not know, or had he just pretended not to? She is besieged by a thought—a malicious thought, very unlike her: Andreas is trying to get away, all of this is a lie, nothing but an excuse to escape her. Is this really happening? Is she going to turn up at his house and he won't be there? He will spend hours away, supposedly working, while she paces, hot with desire, waiting for him? Silently, she digs around in the dirt, catches a worm with her fingers, red, shiny, and wet. She is so taken aback that it doesn't even disgust her. She lets it crawl over her hand.

The new job means they see a lot less of each other than before. Andreas is scheduled to work mornings only, but sometimes—with increasing frequency—he's gone the whole afternoon. Nat continues to go to him at the end of the day, when it's getting dark. They go to bed, they have dinner, then she goes back to sleep at her own house, scrupulously observing what now constitutes a norm. He barely tells her anything about what he does in Petacas, about his work, and she doesn't ask; she doesn't want to seem nosy or dumb, and a strange caution—strange but understandable—leads her to choose silence. They talk, sure, about other things, usually in bed or while making dinner, but it is conversation that tiptoes, beating around the bush. As days go by, a new habit emerges: they have dinner first, then go to bed. Nat registers the change with disappointment and a pain that is slight but sharp. To her, it signals the loss of the urgency that possessed them both in the beginning;

SARA MESA

desire so pressing, so fierce, that it did not tolerate delay. Now, Nat thinks, the hunger for food is greater than the hunger for their bodies.

Andreas's distance weighs so heavily on her that she believes she cannot bear it. She is completely incapable of translating, and the idle hours become fodder for suspicion. In an effort to stave off those thoughts, she offers to give old Joaquín a hand looking after his wife and their house. They quickly come to an agreement: Nat will visit a couple of times a week and will also bring them their daily shopping. On workdays, she will help Joaquín bathe Roberta, wash the floors and dishes, do the laundry, and cook for them. They can't pay much, but something is better than nothing.

She also goes to Píter's to distract herself. They easily resume their early sociability, although now, in order to avoid particular subjects, they stick to trivial conversation and amuse themselves with movies or word games, the kind of humor that makes Nat laughs like a little girl. Contrary to what she might have expected, Píter doesn't reproach her for having abandoned her intellectual labor—the translation he'd praised so highly—for the dull and utilitarian work of looking after an old couple. In fact, he approves of her decision because it speaks to her idea of community. Nat doesn't know if this is a sincere opinion or if he just wants to placate her, but she is conscious of the fact that her friends in Cárdenas, or her family, would not bear to see her like this, a cleaning lady, *the help*, as her mother used to say. Is this where your studies have gotten you? they would ask. Waiting around for a man she barely knows like a bitch in heat, bathing a half-mad old lady, sleeping alone, her only companion a dog she still has to tie up at night? What kind of life has she chosen? Were these the ends of all her supposed rebelliousness?

One day, she gets carried away and falls glibly into confessional mode. She tells Andreas what she told Píter the first night she had dinner at his house. The story of the job she quit. The motiveless theft. Her rejection of compassion and reprieve, her pointless pride. It is, perhaps, Andreas's mute response that paradoxically encourages her to continue speaking, to use words that are progressively imprecise and spacious, words like *guilt, absence, confusion, vertigo.* Andreas makes no reply and she keeps talking, lost in abstraction, lying on her back, staring at the ceiling, at the naked light bulb she knows like the back of her hand, that dusty bulb and black wire.

Only when she stops talking is the weight of his silence evident—the stale air, Li purring at their feet—and Nat becomes conscious of Andreas's slow breathing, his stillness beside her. Suddenly, everything—the bedroom, the cat, her own body—seems unreal to her, toy-like, small and insignificant. She even thinks he might have fallen asleep, but his eyes are open and vacant, indecipherable.

"What do you think about all of that?" she asks.

"All of what?"

"What I told you. You're so quiet. What are you thinking about?"

Andreas sits up and gives her a hard look, there is a new opacity in his eyes—glass eyes, dead eyes. His voice is dry, unexpectedly severe.

"Are you just asking to ask, or do you really want to know?"

For an instant, Nat thinks he's joking, but when his inert eyes and creased chin do not soften, she knows he is not joking, not one bit.

"Have you ever stopped to think about other peoples' lives? About the actual worries people have?"

"What? How is that related to . . ."

"It's related. It's totally related."

Like a child ordered to parrot back what someone has just explained, Andreas repeats her story. In his voice, in his words, it all sounds flimsy, a triviality bordering on the grotesque: she had a good job, she stole something without knowing why—something that, supposedly, she didn't need—she was forgiven for her mistake, but even so, she chose to quit her job and come to La Escapa, where she ended up with another job, after all, because now she goes to the old couple's house and they pay her for it. Is that right?

"Yeah, more or less," Nat says coolly.

"And you think you have a right to complain?"

"Complain? That's not . . . You've misunderstood."

"Don't you know there are people who steal out of necessity? Who lose their jobs without the slightest justification? That this happens to people every day? That they get fired because of a simple oversight? They forgave you and you're still complaining?"

"I'm not complaining! I was talking about something else!"

"What were you talking about, then?"

But she doesn't know how to respond. The man lying beside her, the naked man with whom she has just exploded in pleasure, is now an armed stranger. He, who never gets upset, speaks then of his mother, as if he needed to get angry in order to expose an intimate piece of himself. He tells her that she was Kurdish, from northern Iraq. When she was very young, she was forced to flee from war—one of many—and go into exile in Turkey, traveling on foot for days and nights with a baby—him—in her arms. Later, she suffered hunger and hardship in Germany—he'll spare her the miserable details—and still, he says, his mother never stole anything. She was a good woman, brave and generous. She never spoke a word of complaint.

"I'm sorry," Nat whispers.

"What are you sorry for? That my mother's suffered or that you've been complaining about nothing?"

"I'm sorry about your mother. But it seems like you're blaming me. My story has nothing to do with hers."

"Nobody said anything about blame. It's simply a matter of being grateful. As soon as you get your hands on something, you're already thinking about what elsse you can snatch."

"What are you talking about?"

"I mean in general. That's how you are."

"You don't know me that well! How can you say that?"

"You asked me what I thought. You said you wanted to know. Well, that's what I think. Don't take it as an attack. I mean, they're just my thoughts."

Nat is going to cry. An ungrateful cry-baby? That's what Andreas thinks of her? Is that really how she is and never realized? She deeply regrets having spoken because she has fallen back, lost points. Andreas has seen a part of her that repulses him. And she's going to lose him because of it.

She feels an abyss open on the bed between them.

They drive up El Glauco, in Andreas's van. It was his suggestion—it's Sunday, his day off—a proposal Nat interprets as recognition that there is something between that goes beyond the walls of his bedroom. It's odd, being with him outdoors. All of a sudden, to be out walking with him seems more intimate than being in his bed or undressing in front of him. She is profoundly shaken, as well, by the feeling of him beside her, driving. She shudders with desire when he changes gears—his fist around the gearshift, the fingers that touch her occupied now with another instrument. She admires his profile, his droopy glasses, the line of his dour, proud nose. She allows herself to be swept up in a fierce, gluttonous joy, though she simultaneously tries to brake; by now, she can recognize the kind of joy that ends in anguish. Like when your legs quit after a long run, she thinks.

They take a very narrow dirt road which ends at a lookout point. They leave the van parked and climb the last stretch, up a steep and slippery slope flanked by thorny bushes that snag on their clothes. Nat's calves get scratched, she feels tiny insects swarming around her head, a constant and maddening buzz, she is out of breath and tired. At no point does Andreas hold out his hand to her. He walks a few meters ahead, determined, never once looking back. Nat's elation has completely dissipated and she wonders what they were missing by being there. In a different time, they wouldn't have wanted to leave the bed, they wouldn't have wasted the hours like this. Do they need field trips now?

But the effort is worth it. From up above, Nat takes in a view she never could have imagined, the fields around La Escapa studded with little white and dun-brown cottages, farmhouses, farms, a broken stream that glimmers in some places. The beauty of distance, she thinks, and allows herself to imbibe the scent of the mountain, the hawthorn and elderberry, the rosemary. They kiss and he strokes her cheek.

"You're beautiful," he says.

Nat looks at him, suddenly grateful. But Andreas's eyes are already absent, distant behind the lenses of his glasses, and the buzzing continues around her head, as though it came from the middle of her brain. A few kestrels circle overhead; Andreas squints to make them out. They're hunting, he says. They can stay like that for minutes, soaring until they spot prey, he murmurs to himself. They look down over the edge of a steep drop off and she thinks: we're alone, he could push me and make me fall, leave me out here, injured, with no chance of getting back, nobody knows I'm here, nobody would miss me. The thought is a blunt assault, as if it hadn't come from her. Maybe, because the attack comes from the outside, is the reason it feels so plausible, so near.

Andreas offers her water from the canteen.

"It's cold," he says. "You need it."

Has he sensed her fear? Grateful again, Nat drinks, and as she drinks she feels like she is being cleansed, that the water washes the poison of foreboding from her throat. She is on the verge of apologizing to him, but what for. He would never understand.

Nat had almost completely forgotten about the landlord by the time he next makes his next appearance at her house. He looks at her as usual, staring at her body—her breasts—making a show of his power and boorishness. Nat doesn't have the cash on hand. She usually stocks up at the ATM in Petacas, but forgot this time. She apologizes. She tells him she's been very busy with work. She didn't expect him so soon. Time is flying. He looks at her sideways, purses his lips until they disappear.

"Well, your buddy goes to Petacas every day. He could have gotten money out for you."

Her buddy: an oblique allusion, tainted, which Nat cannot respond to.

None of this would happen if he would just let her transfer him the money like everybody else does. Or at least warn her before he shows up, not like this, out of the blue, waving the water and electric bills, as if she had nothing better to do than wait around with the exact amount of cash in an envelope. But she will only think of these arguments later. What predominates now is the landlord's expression. His lips thinning in a sneer. The glint in his eyes. Arms crossed, smug.

Nat apologizes again and tells him to wait a minute. She turns away and calls Píter to ask for the money she needs. She speaks quietly, but the landlord overhears their conversation.

"Got them eating right out of your hand," he grumbles.

Píter is at her disposal. If she wants, he'll run the money over right now. Nat hesitates a moment. She doesn't want him witnessing the way the landlord speaks to her, how he imposes his humiliating conditions.

"No, don't worry. I'll come to you," she says, and hangs up.

Then, mustering the courage, she asks the landlord to come back in a little bit. Fifteen, twenty minutes max.

"I won't be long."

"I better stay here, that way I can rest."

Nat tries, unsuccessfully, to speak. Her head is starting to spin. The landlord laughs.

"What, you don't trust me?"

He sits down on the couch and looks around the room with a tight smile on his face, observing everything, intending for her to see him do it. Nat doesn't argue. She rushes out.

"I'll be right back," she says again.

She is still shaking when she returns. The landlord indulgently counts the bills, then sticks them in his shirt pocket after folding them slowly. Nat senses the house is steeped in his smell, an acrid odor, unpleasant, hanging heavy in the air. When he leaves, she checks that he hasn't touched anything. Everything appears to be in order, except, perhaps, a couple of magazines he must have thumbed through. Her bedspread is wrinkled, but it maybe it had already been like that, she can't remember. She tosses the magazines in the trash, throws the bedspread in the washing machine on hot, and spends the rest of the afternoon cleaning, the windows open, airing things out.

Despite the minimal attention she now pays him, Sieso is much changed. Nat no longer ties him up at night and he repays her trust with loyalty, sleeping on the floor beside her bed. Maybe she should start thinking about changing his name, she thinks. For as ironic and even affectionate as she intended it to be, the meaning of *sieso* is bad-tempered, rude, a nasty piece of work. And the vet already warned her: animals don't understand irony.

On the other hand, she thinks, maybe it isn't worth it. Most people don't even know that meaning. As a sort of insult, the term *sieso* is only used in certain spaces and circles; its usage is much more limited than Nat initially believed. She thought it was a well-known adjective because she knew it, frequently used because she used it frequently. She wasn't aware of its limitations until she realized even Píter didn't know what it meant. Later, she confirmed that its colloquial meaning isn't even included in the dictionary. The entry lists only the scientific definition, much more unpleasant than she'd expected: "From the Latin *sessus* 'seat' 1. Noun. Anus with the inferior portion of the rectum."

But if nobody knows, then who cares?

It's just a dog's name.

Li paces around the house, unsettled, her meows sounding different, deep and pitiful. Nat observes her, notices that she had recently grown fatter. Could she be pregnant? she wonders. Later, she asks Andreas. He chuckles.

"Wouldn't be the first time. When my ex-wife left her with me, she promised the cat was spayed. But here she is, getting chunky again."

Nat is stricken. His ex-wife? Has she heard him correctly? The wind rattles the shutters, warning of the coming storm. The first drops are already plinking off the roof shed and a sudden gloom envelops them. She must not allow that sound and that light—those memories—to be ruined. For something that once meant one thing to come to mean its opposite.

Andreas is fixing the TV connection. The screen on the antiquated set, which they now occasionally watch during dinner, is always beset by wavy lines that distort the image. Perhaps because his back is to her, possibly because he is focused on something else, Nat dares to press.

"So, Li isn't yours?"

"Well, uh, at this rate I don't think anybody is coming to get her."

"I didn't know you were married."

"Well, how would you?" He turns to grab a screwdriver. "That was years ago. Before I moved out here."

"So . . . what happened?"

"What else . . . the usual. We didn't understand each other. She was really young, I was way older, more than twenty years, I think, and she wanted stuff I couldn't give her."

"Like what?"

"Just stuff. I mean, in general. Stuff like trips, kids. Stuff I don't care about. So she got sick of it and left."

Nat sits on the couch and pets Li as she watches him take apart the TV. Li. If the cat wasn't his, if she had belonged to his ex-wife, then the woman had obviously picked the name. Now she understands why Andreas told her it didn't mean anything, when in reality, it meant everything. Why didn't he tell her the truth back then? The stab of jealousy, so swift and unexpected, makes her ashamed: she always thought she was exempt from such a petty feeling. And yet, who pulls the strings of her suffering now? Who decided that something like this—the past of a man she barely knows—could wound her so badly, overshadow her own convictions and ideas?

In a vague way, she feels duped. What led her to accept the roof exchange was a vision of Andreas that is now completely muddled. She was attracted to the impression she had of him—an image he himself might have wanted to convey: a country bumpkin with no possibility for change, a man who hadn't been with a woman—he said so himself!—in a long time. A man who had lost his ability to seduce—if he'd ever had it—and found himself obliged to propose an exchange of goods, as if he lived in a primitive settlement, ignorant of the rules of common decency. A man who perhaps never left the village, and when he did, it was only to haul crates of the vegetables he grew. A crass man, uncultured, who lived in the country since childhood, adapting instinctively to any old turf like an abandoned dog. A man who simply—who only—made one clumsy, humble request: that she *let him enter*, like a beggar on a doorstep. His inexperience had elevated her, made her powerful. His lack was, for her, riches.

But that man has a college degree. He lived in a city for many years. He was once married. Married to a very young—and presumably attractive—woman. He got divorced. He'd followed life's usual path, observed the usual rites. So then why is his way of relating to her so unusual?

The first thunderclap comes as she observes his damp neck, the way he fiddles with the cables. She swallows. What else can she say? He doesn't seem very willing to elaborate.

She focuses on controlling the thoughts that are taking root inside her, to cut off their limbs as best she can. Since she met Andreas, everything has gone completely off-script. Dismantling all of her prejudices, Andreas digs into her defenselessness, removing her confidence by the shovelful. She becomes increasingly small, while he, in contrast, grows stronger. He is freer, she more dependent.

She can't handle another surprise. This is why she is afraid to speak.

That day will be the first that she won't be able to avail herself of desire in order to forget. The first time she must overcome her thoughts as they undress, force herself not to lose heart. The first time her body labors to respond to him and she exaggerates her pleasure, the first time sex becomes something sad, bitter, and oppressive.

Píter opens a bottle of wine and serves her a little, but Nat, preoccupied, is slow to take the glass, as if she didn't quite understand what it contained or why she is holding it.

Píter jokes, tries to lighten her mood. Weakly, she follows along. What was very funny before—his silly jokes—she now finds dull or just plain stupid. Why is she there, in his house? Just to kill time before she goes to Andreas? Píter inspects her closely. Is everything okay? Yeah, fine, Nat says, all good, but her tight smile tells a different story.

To confess her malaise, she thinks, would be to validate a prediction that Píter has never actually made. Or has made surreptitiously, which makes it all the more complicated to refute.

If she considers the facts on their own, abstaining from parallel interpretations, objectively she has nothing to complain about. What's she going to say? That Andreas was married? That now he's working in Petacas? That one day—just one time—he accused her of being ungrateful when she asked for his opinion?

To express her pain—her ridiculous pain—out loud would only make her more vulnerable. Yet not talking, keeping it all to herself, doesn't make it go away.

They're sitting on the porch, protected by the glass partition. El Glauco's outline softens in the twilight; soon the darkness will swallow it whole. Nat fixes her eyes on it, the mountain where, not long ago, she and Andreas climbed, trying to keep sight of it in the gloaming. Píter sets out smoked salmon, a plate of cheese and cured meats, spicy potato salad in colorful bowls. He is always so obliging, so sensitive! Andreas has never made her a dinner like this. He wouldn't make it for anybody, not even himself.

Nat gives in, speaking nervously.

"Did you know Andreas was married?"

"Me? How would I know? That guy is practically autistic, he never tells anyone anything. How do you know? Did he tell you?"

"He mentioned it the other day, by chance."

"I seriously doubt that he says or does anything by chance. He must have told you for a reason, looking for something."

Nat is quiet. Better to end the conversation, she thinks, before Píter starts dropping hints. But now that he's taken the bait, he isn't going to let go so easily.

"What did he tell you?"

"Not much. That she was younger. Like, by twenty years."

"Twenty years!" Píter whistles, then laughs. "Check out the German!"

Nat is immensely hurt by that whistle. To hide it, she immerses herself in her glass, knocking back the rest of the wine. She shouldn't have spoken, but there's no taking it back now. The only way to stop the conversation is to invent an excuse, get up, and go.

"Hey, what's wrong? Are you mad?"

Repeatedly she denies it, grabs his hand to prove it, assures him nothing is wrong. But what about dinner? She's going now, without a bite? He doesn't care what she says, it is simply not normal to up and leave like this.

Nat knows it. She knows her behavior is erratic and rude, incomprehensible from the outside, or maybe the opposite, all too transparent. But she can't stop. She's certain she has begun a descent. And her only option is to keep going down.

She wakes at midnight and can't fall back to sleep. She remembers Andreas's words, which now, in the silence, become more and more cutting. *Way older. Stuff she wanted and he couldn't give her. Stuff like trips, kids. Stuff he doesn't care about.*

Nat had come to believe she was powerful compared to Andreas. She liked to think that, at twelve years her senior, he'd been seduced by her youth, that it elevated her, increased her market value. But this had been another miscalculation.

She has always considered it an indisputable fact that men, regardless of their age, are attracted to younger women. But until now, she'd never interpreted that as a threat: no matter how young you are, someone will always be younger. She had never thought in terms of competition. Now she does.

She thinks about the girl from the shop.

Sometimes Andreas drives her to Petacas in his van, where—supposedly—she places orders or collects merchandise ready for pick up. The girl from the shop is very young, practically a teenager, but—by the looks of it—not only doesn't her age present a problem, it's a bonus. Nat remembers the heat Andreas gave off when driving. The desire he can awaken simply by changing gears—the taut forearm and strong fist, gripping the stick shift—his eyes jumping from the rearview mirror to the road, the hard eyes she can never get past.

The shared intimacy of the van, the dense air and cigarette smoke. The girl isn't pretty, but she does exude a seductive audacity and, most importantly, she's dying to escape, she's bored, anxious to try new things. Might he, when the time comes, also ask her if he can *be inside a little while*? Might he have already asked her, maybe even before Nat? If all Andreas needed was a little female warmth, wouldn't the girl also do? Even better, in fact? Did he stop because she was underage? And if she weren't?

Nat can't understand why Andreas offers to drive her to Petacas. Andreas, who is so distant with everyone else, makes an exception for the girl, like supplying the damn store was his responsibility. Nat draws her conclusions and feels cold, an intense cold that radiates from her own insides, from a spot somewhere between her spine and breastbone.

Why is Andreas with her? Because he hasn't found anything better? Because she's what he has on hand?

Once one certainty has crumbled, can't they all come down?

Her internal gaze has turned wary and she can no longer curb it. I'm going crazy, she whispers, and looks with burning eyes around her dark room, a private space that does not protect her, but turns on her, stabs her in the back.

She remembers that recurring dream, the one with the man who entered her house while she was tied, defenseless, to the bed, the man whose face she never manages to see. Maybe he didn't represent the landlord, like she'd thought. Maybe it was an omen of what was to come.

Her relationship with Andreas has been tainted from the beginning. The way it began, a way that once enthralled her, a way that has been turned inside out, showing its repugnant seams.

It's not as though she was innocent and pure before, but at least parts of her—leery, malicious parts—had been dormant. They're awakened now. The damage grows, branches off inside her.

When she is cleaning out the old couple's storage room, Nat finds several boxes of books: mostly schoolbooks and literary classics, but also a few newsstand novels that must have been popular decades ago and which nowadays, nobody remembers. Joaquín explains that Roberta was a teacher for forty years, the better part of them in the elementary school in Petacas. The books are hers, he says, or rather, they were. She hasn't been able to read a single word for a long time now; that's why she's decided to take them off the shelves and pack them away, out of her sight, so they wouldn't torment her.

Nat studies Roberta, so fragile and confined to her own world, so hermetic, and it's hard to imagine her having another life. Roberta, working with kids, going over a lesson on the chalkboard, subject and predicate, addition and subtraction? Nat flips through her books, annotated, underlined, bookmarks made of construction paper and pressed flowers—had Roberta made them? had her students?—and her chest tightens.

What does Roberta think about, what does she look at? She always appears deeply focused on something occurring in another dimension, her eyes, wrinkles, and lips forming silent sentences. Who is she talking to?

Sometimes the spell breaks and the woman comes back to herself. Then she discovers that she isn't alone and tries to be pleasant with the people around her. She might speak nonsense or get frustrated when they don't understand her, but she is a polite woman, and never makes a scene.

One day, Roberta receives a call with dire news. A relative, a nephew perhaps, is dying. This is what Nat deduces from overhearing Roberta converse, eyes lowered, twisting the phone cord around her fingers. Afterward, she spends several hours deep in thought, picking up—then hanging up—the telephone, although no one is calling. When Nat asks Joaquín, he shakes his head and says Roberta has made it all up. There is no sick nephew, nobody is dying. It happens a lot, he says. She gets fixated on things from the past. In the old man's resignation, Nat also senses a hint of despair. What will happen when he isn't there to take care of her?

Joaquín is going blind. He confesses this to her one day, in tears, his head on his fists, seated at the kitchen table. Nat is moved by seeing a man cry, a man that age.

Joaquín and Roberta represent a crack in the community; they are, in a way, as anomalous and defective as Nat. It's hard to see, hard to look beyond, it isn't pleasant. But once she makes the leap, she can no longer feign her innocence.

The afternoon is overcast. The still air is charged with static electricity. Buzzards fly low, soaring over Nat as she walks toward Andreas's house, an unusual direction for this time of day. She knows he isn't home. She doesn't know why she took this route and not another—she hasn't stopped to consider this—just like she doesn't know why she decided to go for a walk, even though it threatens to rain at any moment. Intuition perhaps, a hunch? That's what she will tell herself later when replaying the events. Now she is just walking, her thoughts elsewhere, until his house takes shape in the distance, and there, at the gate, his parked van. She stops. It takes her a moment to comprehend. Or try to comprehend. Her temples pulse wildly, a flash of heat rushes to her face. She turns abruptly on her heel. It's better if no one sees her there.

She gets home and tries to calm herself. There must be some explanation. A reasonable explanation, she thinks: Andreas has returned to La Escapa because something came up, he had to pick up a tool or forgot some equipment. Or maybe, maybe, there's something wrong with the van and he took a different car this morning, got a ride someone else. She feeds Sieso, opens a beer, lies down. But she gets right back up. The explanation could be very different: at that exact moment, *right now*, Andreas could be in his house with another woman. Another woman he's bamboozled with the same ruse he used to bamboozle her.

She leaves her house again and walks quicky—now in the rain—toward the shop, her breathing ragged, until she can look inside and see the girl behind the counter, texting on her phone. Nat's relief at the sight of the girl is so great that she laughs, but her laughter, too, is short-lived: if it isn't the girl, it could be anyone.

Or maybe it's nobody. But if it's nobody, why didn't he call her right away, like they used to? Doesn't he have the urge to see her? Isn't he dying for it like she is?

She spends the whole afternoon walking back and forth between their houses. The van is always in the same place. It hasn't been moved. She just needs to see the white smudge and she turns around, starts a new loop. Her heart is beating so fast that it scares her. She has never done anything like this, not even close. Nothing so grotesque, so undignified.

She lets the phone ring when Andreas calls her that night, ignoring the call until he tires of trying. She would have liked for him to try a little longer, to not give up so easily, but even so, to ignore his calls feels like a secret revenge. She feels she's won, although what battle?

The next time they get together, they both act normally, or what constitutes normal for them now. He doesn't ask why she didn't answer his call. She doesn't ask why his van was parked at his house all day. Since there are no questions, there are no answers. Nat's mistrust continues to grow: subtle and twisted, like a cat's cageyness. And his? If it's mistrust or simple disinterest, she couldn't say.

She makes a habit of spying on him after that. She pokes around the area near his house, watches the van's comings and goings, compares timetables. She scours for indications of possible visitors. Finding nothing, she thinks: he's careful, he destroys the evidence. When Andreas isn't watching, she inspects everything she can get her hands: food jars, medicine, bottles. She keeps track of how many condoms they use and does her math. She examines the papers that lay scattered around the house—invoices, commercial notices, advertising fliers, receipts. She finds some old CD-ROMs and sneaks them out to secretly review at home. Just blueprints and topographical reports, but her anxiety is not quelled, she keeps searching. In his closet, she discovers dress clothes, nicer than what he usually wears—she has never seen him in a suit, but there they are, irrefutable, jackets and ties. Two additional discoveries produce deep misgivings: a receipt from a women's clothing store in Cárdenas—*woman's shirt 39.90 euros*—from two years back—*Thank You For Shopping*—and a little musical jewelry box with a tiny ballerina that, when the lid is open, turns and turns to the tune of "La vie en rose." Nat shuts it, not wanting to give herself away. She wants to smash it.

Snooping on his phone yields few results because he hardly ever uses it. All she finds are texts she's sent him, spam messages, and calls made and received from the same numbers, which belong to his associate in Petacas and some supposed client. The fact that Andreas always leaves his phone out, freely accessible, and that his contacts are so limited might mean there is nothing to fear. But it could also mean the opposite: that Andreas is faking, that while she sneaks around, he is sneaking around too, erasing numbers and compromising messages and leaving the phone within her reach, all to mislead her.

Nat always chooses the worst from all possible interpretations. She's never safe, not even when she convinces herself that her ideas don't make sense. Any variation, any nuance she hasn't foreseen—as slight or remote as it may be—makes her reel. Jealousy, that unrelenting green-eyed monster, slips into bed with them, its pointed tongue and obscene sneers, probing them, ready to devour them, poisoning the meaning of their movements, staining them with baseness and suspicion. Why does Andreas shut his eyes when he's with her? Is it because he's thinking of someone else? Because he's remembering his young ex-wife? His dark eyelids, his concentrated expression and the light tremor of his lashes, everything that Nat admired in the early days, what turned her on, now represents the confirmation of all her suspicions. Nat, threatened with frigidity, has also started to fantasize. She dreams up scenarios in which other men ask her what Andreas asked her. They do the same things to her—exactly the same—that he did the first time, under the same darkness and in the same silence, naked only from the waist down, no caresses except his hands running slowly down her sides. They perform like Andreas, but are not Andreas, because Andreas isn't who he used to be either: he is a different man, a different man who is probably conducting himself as she does, exiling her even as he touches her, pushing her away the deeper he delves into her body. When they finish, they are quiet, not with their earlier shyness, but sadness. Are you cold? he asks, handing her a blanket. You can't imagine how cold, she wants to say, remembering how he used to wrap her in his arms. Now he only wraps her in courtesy, clumsy and hurtful.

She barely ever goes to Petacas now, just quick trips to get money from the ATM, as if the town—already a hostile place—was prohibited to her since Andreas started working there. But one day, consumed by wild conjecture, she decides to go with the excuse of getting a haircut. She tells Andreas ahead of time, in passing, so he doesn't get any ideas if he sees her around town. Andreas looks up, observes her in a way that makes her feel exposed.

"But your hair's fine. Why do you want to cut it?"

"I need a trim. I haven't had it cut in ages."

"I think you look fine."

This comment, which could be considered a compliment, is interpreted by Nat as sign of detachment: Andreas doesn't want her to show up in Petacas, he doesn't want to have her around. But she can't back out now. It would be even weirder to renege: a clear confession.

She goes early and parks in the first spot she finds. Since she doesn't know where a hairdresser is, she ambles along, avoiding the mud collected along the sidewalk. And it's just when she reaches the town hall square that she sees Andreas talking to someone, vigorously waving his arms, as if he were arguing, smoking while speaking, tilting his head back to blow out smoke, legs slightly apart. They are gestures Nat doesn't recognize in him, and even his body, seen from a distance, looks unfamiliar. The man Andreas is talking to is taller than him, and younger. Much younger, actually, which turns Andreas into another person, practically an old man. For a moment, Nat feels an urge to retreat and hide, but she steels herself and walks toward him. As she gets close, she can tell the men are not arguing; they are simply talking the way men talk sometimes, with that mix of sarcasm, camaraderie, and crudeness. He turns, sees her, and smiles. His smile doesn't mean, however, that she is welcome, as he immediately disengages from his interlocutor, as if he didn't want her to come any closer. He doesn't introduce her. He says a quick goodbye to the other man as his smile fades.

"What are you doing here?"

"I'm getting my hair cut, don't you remember?"

"Oh yeah, that's right. Where are you going exactly?"

"Nowhere in particular. I don't know where there's a salon."

"Come on, I'll show you one."

He sets off walking a few steps ahead, glancing around as if looking for somebody else, as if she were the odd one out or as if she weren't even there. Nat follows him with a heavy heart. Andreas hasn't kissed her, obviously, and hasn't come close enough to touch her either, yet just a minute ago, she saw him with his hand clapped on his friend's shoulder.

"Look. Here's where I work."

Though the door of a small establishment, Nat glimpses an office crammed with papers, pieces of equipment, and boxes, with a couple of computers and a giant printer in the center of the room. Andreas's colleague—a man the same age as him, with disheveled hair and wearing a tracksuit—leans over a couple of blueprints so big they drag on the floor. He doesn't seem worried that they might get creased or dirty. Andreas waves to him from the door. He doesn't go inside and doesn't invite her to go in. He raises his arm to point down the street, the hairdresser is that way, he says, two or three blocks down. His tone is so curt—or so it seems to Nat—that it accentuates her interloper status. When he says goodbye, he squeezes her arm and looks her in the eyes, but this isn't enough for Nat now.

She's an outsider at the salon, too. The hairdresser, with her long curly mane, tight T-shirt, and strident laugh, is straightening a client's hair when Nat walks in. The woman doesn't put down her tools or ask what she can do for her; she asks her— orders her, more like—to take a seat and wait. This is what Nat does, wait, while she tries to read a book she's brought. With her eyes glued to the page, she listens to the conversation between the two women, who criticize someone with tacit comments and private jokes. Their complicit laughter makes Nat uncomfortable, as though they were laughing at her, too—and who knows, she thinks, maybe they are. When it's her turn, the hairdresser scrutinizes her in the mirror. She asks how she wants the cut but doesn't pay attention to Nat's instructions. She inspects her hair, lifting clumps and carelessly letting them fall. It's really damaged, she says, a lot needs to come off.

Nat doesn't reply. She lets the woman do what she hasn't asked for.

Now, the new style has added on a few years; she looks even paler and more baggy-eyed than before. Despite telling the woman she didn't want bangs, she now has them, parted in the middle. But she smiles and, without complaint, pays the girl what she asks for.

Before leaving for La Escapa, she stops at the indoor market to shop for the old couple. In line, she observes the chatterbox women and foul-mouthed men, their cryptic way of speaking, at breakneck speed, completely foreign to her. A pair of loose dogs sniff around the boxes undisturbed. She has to keep an eye out because as soon as she's distracted, someone cuts in and takes the best product. Even the children—shouldn't they be in school?—look crafty and sly. And the teenagers have an arrogant glint in their eye, defiant.

It can't be so horrible, she tells herself. It's her, her way of seeing things, that's sick. If only she could shut her eyes and see no more.

She hasn't thought of her in years. But, thanks to the hairdresser episode, it unexpectedly returns: the memory of those luminous days and how they later turned sad and baffling. Nat was seven or eight at the most; Estrella must only have been a few months older, although at that age a difference of a few months constituted a big step, an assurance, since it was a privilege to be the friend—or enjoy the favor—of an older girl.

She can't remember her face or voice, but she does remember how the girl sat behind her, brushing her hair. Estrella dreamed of being a hairdresser, but she couldn't practice on everyone, she said, just her, lucky Nat, chosen from among all the other girls, the one with the softest hair—she claimed—the longest and prettiest of all the locks. She did braids and little buns, she brushed her hair for hours, blew softly on her neck to tickle her, and Nat closed her eyes and let herself be handled.

One day, she started to yank, pull her ponytail much too tight. Your hair's breaking, the girl would say, and she would throw the brush on the floor in a huff. Nat did not understand what mistake she had made, she begged the girl to try again and, if she hurt her, she silently held back her tears. In a couple of days, Estrella had replaced her. From her corner, Nat watched her brushing the chosen girl's hair, combing with extreme care, tying it back with colorful elastics, doing little braids around her forehead—things she had never done with her—taking the girl's chin to admire the finished product, joyfully clapping her hands. The new girl observed Nat from afar, a little uncomfortable, perhaps, but helplessly gratified.

Nat didn't know what sin she had committed to be punished like that. When she saw a picture of Adam and Eve expelled from Eden, she thought: that's what's wrong with me.

Her neighbors are unloading bags of food from their minivan while the kids run around, dragging a bow and quiver of colored arrows. Despite the fog and distance, Nat has the impression that the wife is pregnant. The man waves and she feels obliged to go over, to be polite. They ask how her week has been. They complain about the storm, the wind that took down the thatching on the porch roof. They are unexpectedly cordial again, affectionate even. As if she's only interesting when they can smell trouble, she thinks. As if they sensed that things were falling apart for her and were happy about it.

The woman takes her arm and, yes, she confesses, she's pregnant. Her eyes shine as she says it, grabbing Nat with the closeness one uses with female friends, and invites her over for dinner that very night. To celebrate, she says. Before Nat can reply, the woman changes her tone and lowers her voice. Stroking her belly, she adds: the invitation is just for you. Nat doesn't understand at first.

"I mean . . . we wouldn't like it if the German came."

"Andreas?"

"That's right, Andreas."

"Of course," Nat nods. "No problem."

The wind picks up, cold and biting, almost hygienic. A draft that puts an end to the possibility of rebutting, or at least asking. A draft that draws the conversation back to the weather, what a pain. But Nat wonders: why the prohibition?

Going to dinner will mean not seeing Andreas that night. Accepting the invitation will then become a message to him, a covert message whose contents aren't clear, even to Nat. She decides not to do any explaining. She simply sends him a text to let him know; they'll see each other tomorrow, she writes.

How will he interpret that offense? The most likely thing, Nat thinks, is that he won't interpret it at all.

That night, during dinner—with Píter also in attendance—the neighbors detail their plans to build a pool on their property. They've run the numbers and it's not that expensive. They want a long and narrow pool, so they'll be able to swim comfortably. A functional pool, even if it isn't pretty.

"The worst thing about a pool is maintaining it," Nat says. "A nightmare."

They nod, they've considered all the drawbacks, but they're still going to put one in.

"I don't know," Nat says. "I've always thought they weren't worth it. Sorry, but I think it's ridiculous, so much water wasted every year . . ."

"You don't drain the water every time. There are products to keep it clean. Products and covers."

"Yeah, harsh chemical products . . . I'm not into them, either."

Nat is being silly and she knows it. She knows nothing about pools yet here she is giving her opinion. What's wrong with her? Does discussing pool maintenance help her contain her urge to get out of there and run straight to Andreas? Píter comes to her rescue and changes the subject; she focuses on her meal and recalls her neighbor's words, her attitude—the lowered gaze, the hesitation in her voice, her hand rubbing her belly—*we wouldn't like it if the German came.* Myriad possibilities flood her mind. It occurs to her that Andreas might have had some kind of run in with the neighbors. Or maybe just with the wife, something private, something inti-mate. After all, she made that plea when her husband wasn't in earshot. He wouldn't have asked her to *let him enter* . . . Her face tightens with pain. Píter watches her from across the table. No, she tells herself, couldn't be. The neighbor used the plural—*we wouldn't like*—so that can't just be the reason. She could ask Andreas himself, eliminate her doubts the easy way. But she won't do that. Andreas is not the least bit af-fected by what other people think of him. If she tells him what happened, he'll just say it doesn't matter, or might not say anything at all. He would never get mad, even if he knew they were going around speaking ill of him. Or letting slip insidious insinuations.

Nothing is more out of character for Andreas than anger. Nat has never seen him get worked up or lose his cool, like she just did over the subject of the pool. He doesn't raise his voice, not even the day he talked about his mother. And he never ar-gues. When he expresses his point of view, he gives it without her need—her yearning—to be understood. Inside him, there is no desire to convince.

Strangely, such an attitude makes Nat more uneasy than the alternative.

Sometimes she wonders if that neutrality is not also an in-visible mode of attack.

They're in bed when they hear Li meowing. The meows are deep, long laments. The cat circles through the house, entering and exiting the bedroom, caterwauling incessantly. Nat's thoughts are miles away and she senses that Andreas's head is also somewhere else. But the noise isn't the only reason. Something in their bodies has ceased to work and cannot be repaired. They go slow, are stiff and awkward in their movements. Nat thinks about how different it was just a few weeks ago, when they held each other and everything was liquid and flowing. That thought—that comparison—makes the situation worse. And then there's the cat, the plaintive cat wailing like a baby—more maddening than a wailing baby—ceaseless, demanding, much more intense than normal, much more insistent. Nat stops.

"Could she be in labor?"

"No," Andreas says. "She's looking for the babies. They were born yesterday."

Nat sits up. Leaning over him, she looks at his face. He isn't wearing his glasses. He looks vulnerable, but distant.

"Well, where are they?"

"I drowned them in a water barrel."

"You drowned them?"

"What was I supposed to do? It was best for them."

Nat is horrified. Why drown them? Was there no other option? He didn't even consider another option! Why couldn't he keep them? He has more than enough space! Or give them away? Doesn't he regret having killed them? Doesn't he feel the slightest compassion? As she asks him all of this, she gets dressed, making a show of her indignation, though she herself knows that the dead kittens aren't her only reason for being upset. Andreas doesn't answer. He gives her a long look of contempt before asking her if this is how the night's going to end, if she's just going to leave in the middle of things, isn't capable of controlling herself at least a little. As if he cares how the night ends, Nat retorts: he's the most insensitive person she has ever come across. Not only when he's killing babies, but always. When she leaves, he'll probably just start watching TV like nothing happened.

He stares at her, undaunted, pupils vacant. He slowly gets dressed, carefully puts on his glasses before speaking. The end is foretold in every one of his movements. In the way he ties his bootlaces. In how he buckles and then adjusts his belt. In looking up at Nat, bringing her into focus, repeating the words she's just said, *killing babies*, what bunk. She thinks she has the ability to understand and the right to judge. But she doesn't know anything, he says. She should shut up a bit. Take a look around and shut up.

Nat bites her lip, holding back tears.

"You sound like my landlord. The same disrespect. You both think you're better than everyone."

"Because your landlord's right. We have different rules out here. And you don't understand them. It's not as if you don't accept them—you're incapable of understanding them."

"What rules? What rules are you talking about? Trading labor for sex, for example?"

She doesn't have time to regret it. She's said it and it is unforgiveable. Andreas pushes her away with his arm, looks at her harshly. From the edge of the bed, he sighs deeply, smooths his hair, and says, with complete calm, that he wants to split.

"Split *what*?" Nat asks, shaking.

"Split up. End whatever this is between us. Break up. Whatever you want to call it."

"I didn't even know there's was anything between us!"

"No? What do you call coming to my bed every night?"

"I've been asking myself the same thing: what is this?"

"You've never gotten it, have you? That's why you spy on me, circling my house to see if I'm home or not . . . Because you just don't get it."

"What are you talking about?"

"You know what I'm talking about. It's over. You've exhausted my patience."

Nat hears the words without catching them. She perceives the sounds but doesn't grasp them. Something has started to change inside her. Her rage dissolves and makes way for a hollow whose echo thunders throughout her entire body. She has fallen into a well and is drowning. She rubs her eyes with her fists, looking at him from a distinctly different place now. Her voice—her own voice—sounds remote to her, as if she were a dummy, speaking words that come from very far away, outside herself.

"No, no, no. You're not serious."

Andreas doesn't answer. A profound stillness takes her over: she is out of the game. She stays a little longer, paralyzed, now sitting on the floor, one shoe on and one shoe off, her blouse still unbuttoned, waiting.

"You better go," Andreas says after a few minutes.

Nat stands up, finishes getting dressed, and leaves.

Or rather, she must have stood up, gotten dressed, and left: later, she won't remember doing it, like she was sleepwalking. Neither will she remember what she says when she goes—if she says anything at all—nor how she walks back; how, because of the darkness, she almost has to feel her way forward, stumbling; how she opens her front door, throws herself face down on the bed and grinds down into the mattress, attempting to suffocate her suffering.

Sieso comes to the edge of the bed, rubs his muzzle gently against her face, then lies down on the rug beside her. Now, with the exception of that dog—the guardian of the dead—she is alone, completely alone. Surrounded only by silence: the usual fictitious silence. A four-wheeler's engine drills the air, a couple of dogs bark in the distance, and coming toward her, some new words make their way: *time is the punishment.*

She speaks them aloud as if she was reading them, as if they didn't come from her, but from beyond, way, way beyond.

III

She calls him the next day, and the next, and the next, refusing to believe that he will keep ignoring her, promising herself every time that this call will be the last, conscious that she's playing into his hands, basely kneeling before him; even so, she persists, she's prepared to show up at his house, appear at his office in Petacas if necessary. Andreas answers on the third day, only to reiterate his decree: they must stop seeing each other. He says it calmly, surely. He doesn't get upset. He doesn't yell. He doesn't admonish her for the previous calls, the harassment. Her doesn't admonish her for anything. In the absence of hysterics, Nat knows his decision is irreversible.

But she cannot accept defeat. She begs. Pleads. He cuts her off. From now on, he will never answer another of her calls or reply to any texts. Andreas's resolve, his coherence, Nat thinks, resides in that: not letting his arm be twisted, not going back on his word.

The knowledge that he has reached his limit makes her literally sick. She gets into her bed and doesn't leave it for days. She keeps her phone close, checks it every five minutes, stashes it under her pillow and feels around for it, overcome with fatigue but never quite falling asleep. Her skin burns with despair, refusing to admit it has lost Andreas, his body, everything they did and will never do again. She goes over what happened again and again, the words they spoke, the order in which they said them. He shoved her away—pushed her with his arm, almost knocking her to the floor—he expelled her from his house. It's so horrible, so heartrending, that she wants to scream at the memory of it.

Píter comes to see her. He is worried about her confinement. What's wrong? Has she been to the doctor? Does she need something? Nat doesn't waver, she won't let her arm be twisted either. She just asks that he explain to the old couple that she can't look after them for a while and that he buy some food for Sieso. How ironic, she thinks: Píter will take charge of feeding the dog he detests.

He must have mentioned her state to the neighbors, because the wife stops by to say hello on Friday. She brings a selection of herbal teas neatly presented in a wooden box, each infusion recommended for a different ill. Chamomile, lemon balm and linden blossom, sage, thyme, valerian and mint, easy remedies for digestive issues, insomnia, aching bones, menstrual pain, even sadness.

"The box is for you. You can keep it, it's a present."

A malicious present, Nat thinks, a suggestion that she will eventually be afflicted by all those maladies, but she thanks her for the gift. The neighbor makes light of it. That's what they're there for, she says, to help each other; she knows that

Nat would do the same if the situation were reversed. Nat observes the burgeoning bump under the neighbor's indigo cotton dress. She looks at the woman as if seeing her for the first time and notices how much more attractive she is than when they met; her hair is silkier, her skin more youthful, she displays a natural elegance that suddenly makes Nat feel very uncomfortable. Almost unwittingly, she asks her point-blank:

"What's up with you and Andreas? What's your problem?"

It sounds much ruder than she would like. An aggressive question, she thinks: now the woman will feel attacked and won't give her an answer. But the neighbor bows her head as if carefully considering the question. But when she looks up, she denies it with a smile.

"Nothing. Nothing is up."

"But you forbade me from bringing him to your house!"

She keeps smiling, unruffled.

"'Forbade' is a bit intense. I just asked you."

"But why?"

Again she pats her belly, swaying.

"No reason. I just don't really know him."

The husband comes to visit in the afternoon. He offers to bring her whatever she needs, do whatever she needs. Is her appearance really that concerning? Or do they suspect the real reason and delight in her pain?

The husband's voice harbors an inappropriate, hopeful note. Does his wife know that he's there? Did she send him, or did he think of it on his own? Nat stares at him and notices how he dithers, as if he wanted to say more than he does, with his liquid—liquified—eyes and a few meaningfully prolonged seconds.

The neighbor doesn't know how to smile without including a smirk of deceit. Or if not deceit, of slyness. For a moment, Nat thinks that they're both of the same stripe.

She has nightmares that leave her exhausted. Sometimes, all she has to do is drift off for a few moments, any time of day or night, for a whole host of beings to appear in her dreams—faceless people, talking animals—to address her, order her about, or lock her up in dark, labyrinthine places. When she wakes, she looks around her and the bedroom seems completely foreign. Every piece of furniture, every object, is in its place, yet something has changed. She can sense it in the atmosphere, like a slight dip in temperature, or the fading colors of an old photograph. As though the world had decided to keep moving forward, mutating, while she has been left definitively behind.

She hates the house so much! How fruitless her efforts to improve it! Her attempts to make her mark through cleaning and decorating have been futile. Her belongings sit there as if they'd been cut and pasted from somewhere else, a poorly executed collage. She looks at the table with her papers, laptop, and books, at the curtains she sewed for the kitchen, the old copper candle holders—so lovely—the ceramic fruit bowl. All of it grates. Everything has grated from the beginning, she tells herself: she does not belong to that place, she has never belonged.

Two full weeks have passed. It's another Sunday. Now it's her turn to make a move, though she doesn't know which move to make, nor in which direction.

She goes out for a walk.

She turns onto the dirt trail that leads to the old couple's house, a trail of orchards and fenced-in plots with chickens and pigs. She can make out the two of them in the distance, sitting under the arbor where grapes are still growing fat. She has abandoned them, she hasn't even stopped in to see how they are doing. Should she? Yes, she should, but later. She contemplates the blossoming orange trees. Unheard of, Píter explained to her, such late flowering, the result of that autumn's unusual heat. Nat wouldn't call it heat herself, but atmospheric stagnation, as if the air had stopped circulating, fossilized at mid-height, not around her feet or face, but at her hips, impeding her progress.

She is alone. Sieso followed her for a couple hundred meters, then stopped in the middle of the path, watching her as she pressed on, ignoring her whistles, before heading back with his ungainly trot. Now Nat approaches the orange trees, discovers that their leaves are plagued with aphids. Some, completely infested with the critters, curl up over themselves, dried out. The pale sky, as good as dirty, is yellowed from a column of smoke that rises in the distance. It smells like smoke and orange blossom and also like dung, all mixed together. A little further on is the incestuous siblings' house with its red graffiti, GOD'S PUNISHMENT and SHAME. Nat peeks through the window openings—the frames stripped and panes removed—and into the interior, which is filled with trash and flies. She enters the dwelling even though she knows there's nothing to see—nothing good—and there, inside those walls where the air is thick, she is overwhelmed by an unbearable conviction. Her actions are futile, it doesn't matter what move she makes: she will never get Andreas back.

She has lost him.

She had him and she lost him.

That certainty rends every single muscle in her body. She believes she will die of pain, she believes it is possible to die like this, alone, among the ruins of that house. She almost falls to her knees, but she contains herself. Leaning against the wall, she tries to control her breath. She has the sense that she's witnessing the last scene of her life. This is true suffering, she thinks. Something terrible is going to happen, she thinks next.

A little later, on the way back home, she detects the commotion: initially, a few figures, out of focus, and then people standing around, huddled around something, the dust cloud raised by a couple of cars—the neighbors' minivan starting up—and shouts muffled by the distance. She quickens her pace as a dark premonition burgeons inside her. She keeps moving, although she doesn't fully understand, even if now the cries belong to specific people; they belong to the neighbor woman jumping into the moving vehicle and to the little boy, throwing a tantrum at being left behind. There is, in addition, a group of two or three men; one of them holds a stick—something that looks like a stick—and prowls Nat's property. The minivan is already gone, its shape almost indiscernible in the dust. What's wrong, she wonders as she hurries, what's happening, then she sees one of the men running toward her, calling to her, his tone is not one of warning, but accusation, as if she were guilty of something, hey, he says, hey! he yells, and all the rest comes very quickly. It's the dog, they say, that savage animal. Where was she? The girl's face is wrecked, they say. Why was her dog running loose? Doesn't she know he's a beast? And where is the devil now? She has to turn him over, they say, they'll make short work of him, that poor girl, she should see her, see what her dog has done. Nat struggles to follow. She looks at the boy, who stands at the door, holding his face in his hands—fingernails scraping his cheeks—screaming in terror, and she sees a woman—the shop owner's wife—picking him up and carrying him off by force. Someone orders her to get out of there, get out of there right now, go find the beast, get out of the way if she doesn't want someone to kill her then and there, at least disappear until that poor woman knows her daughter is out of danger, that pregnant mother, the mother whose little girl's face has been destroyed and whose misfortune, it would appear, is all Nat's fault.

She shuts herself away in her house again, if it can even be called hers, even called a house. She doesn't have a choice, where else can she go? Wherever she might be, whatever she might say, she will be met with repudiation. Píter is the only person to come to see her. He regards her with concern, narrowing his eyes. Nat is wrapped up on the couch, staring blankly at the wall, pupils fixed. Píter tries to raise her spirits, but she only half-listens. The girl's injuries, it seems, weren't that serious, he says. She'll have scars, but there's always plastic surgery. Píter explains something about the cheeks, or one cheek in particular. Across from her, his own face is divided by a shadow. Nat only sees half of his countenance. Píter looks much younger to her now, with his messy beard and cheekbones softened by the gloom, or maybe it's her, maybe she's aged and is seeing him from another era. His voice, low and soothing, continues to explain what Nat cannot grasp at the moment. How tiresome it is to listen when you have nothing to add, she thinks vaguely. Was this what happened to Andreas when she used to talk to him? Is this how her blather made him feel?

"Anyway, you should go out and offer to help. Ask how the kid is doing. She's only six, poor thing."

"Poor thing," Nat repeats. And then: "It's not my fault."

"No, of course it isn't." Píter grabs her hand, gives it a squeeze.

"Everybody hates me now."

"They don't hate you. But you need to cooperate. You can't refuse."

Cooperating means handing Sieso over as soon as he turns up. To be put down. The dog—clever beast—ran away and still hasn't shown any signs of life. Is he capable of understanding what he's done, of anticipating the consequences?

The men of La Escapa, accompanied by a couple of local cops from Petacas, are scouring the area in search of the animal. They've made it as far as El Glauco and are prepared to climb to the top if necessary. The shop owner is the leader of the expedition. He is the most outraged, the most rabid of them all, as if his own daughter had been bit. Nat can still hear the insults he slung at her. The gypsy was the only man who defended her. Leave the girl alone, he said. But then he joined the others in combing the fields.

The idea of putting the dog down horrifies her. She thinks that killing him will only deepen the tragedy. Not the girl's tragedy, not the girl's parents' tragedy, not even Nat's own, but the tragedy of the world in general, a kind of irreversible doom, as though the sacrifice of an animal—of that animal—would forever alter the order of things.

Píter is adamant. "Don't you realize he's dangerous? That he could do the same thing to someone else?"

"She was the one who hopped the fence without permission and came in to play. Sieso wouldn't have attacked if she hadn't climbed over. Besides, where were her parents? Isn't it their fault for leaving her alone?"

Píter stands up, agog, scandalized.

"Don't say that! Don't you ever think about saying that to anyone! You're courting disaster!"

"More disaster?"

"You're in shock. You don't know what you're saying."

Nat nods. She allows him to come close to her, cover her with a blanket.

"You need to rest. I'll come back tomorrow."

The silence is different this time, theatrical, as if all of La Escapa was performing just for her, deception their singular aim. Everybody should be asleep, but there's no way anyone is sleeping. Nat imagines the men of La Escapa out looking for the dog. Looking for him with hunting rifles and sticks, stalking, ready to lynch him as soon as he's found. Are they going to kill him just like that, cruelly, paying him back for all the damage he has done? She dozes off, sinks into a feverish torpor. She dreams about torches, flames glittering, flickering in the distance. And she dreams about Andreas, his hands touching her, caressing her, appearing and disappearing. When she wakes, ochre light is seeping through the blinds. Several hours must have passed, although to her it feels like minutes. She hears a whine behind the door—a soft whine, gentle, almost human. Something is scratching at the wood. She leaps up, opens it. Sieso is on the threshold, looking her directly in the eyes. His coat is filthy and he has a new wound on his leg, but his gaze is clearer than ever. It's a miracle that he made it there without being seen. A genuine miracle, she thinks. Why kill such a creature?

There's no escape. They'd be intercepted the second she started the car—and she would be lynched, too. Even if she stays inside, goes days and days without showing her face, the moment they hear Sieso bark they will break the windows, break down the door like they did to the incestuous siblings, capture them in situ, there will be no escape. Like a cornered animal, she thinks, that's how they've got her. Like Sieso, who is still watching her and whimpering.

There's only one solution. Píter. He can help her. She can still try. She can convince him if she uses the exact right words, convince him how important the dog's salvation is for them all—the entire community. She calls him on the phone and asks him to come as quick as he can, without revealing the reason to hurry.

Píter is struck dumb when he enters her house and sees Sieso there. His eyes swing between Nat and the dog, expectantly. Nat bursts into speech. Has he brought the car? Yes? He can take Sieso in secret, no one will suspect him. Drop him off at a pound. Or anywhere else, in another village. Go as far away as necessary. If the dog stays in La Escapa, they will beat him to death.

"You're crazy," Píter interrupts.

But Nat keeps speaking. Imagine if it was his dog, she says. He wouldn't give it a chance to redeem itself? Even the most despicable criminal is afforded a defense. Has he forgotten what he told her about the snub-nosed adder? That all you had to do was move it away? She grabs him by the shoulders, shakes him. He's always said that he's her friend. Her real friend. He told her to come to him if she needed help. That's precisely what she's doing now. Why can't he support her?

"Because what you're asking me to do is insane. Not only is it *not* in your interest, it's to your detriment! You're upset and you don't understand. You'll thank me in time."

Nat is enraged. Now he's rejecting her too? Is he aligned with the others, now that she's the weakest piece on the board?

"It's about safety. And justice. You can't fight it," he adds.

Nat turns her back, looks away, orders him out of her house. Píter shuffles out. But he isn't the condemned one, she thinks, who does he think he is, walking like that, so dramatic? Surely, he must be satisfied his predictions have borne out. That dog will only bring trouble, he said. It had sounded like a curse, and here is the result.

And maybe it is this correct prediction that gives Píter the authority to turn her in. It must've been him, since within the hour, two police officers are knocking on her door.

Nat can't stop them from taking Sieso. Resistance is futile.

Joaquín comes to her door, glumly wringing his hands. Nat invites him in, but he would rather stay outside, not cross the threshold. With lowered eyes he tells her that it's better if she doesn't work for them for a while.

"At least until things calm down," he adds.

Nobody would understand, he says. They get along with everyone, they have to avoid conflicts that could impact Roberta's health. Nat doesn't argue. She even admits that he's right. The dog bit the girl, the dog belonged to her, so she is guilty. It's justice. There's nothing more to say, nothing to discuss.

Joaquín apologizes again. The blush of embarrassment is visible on his cheeks.

"It's nothing against you. When all of this passes, you can come back."

She sees Roberta that same evening, resting on the porch in the tatty striped deck chair where she usually gets her fresh air. The old woman signals for her to come near. Nat hesitates, she doesn't want to harm her or disobey her husband's orders, but finally she leans on the fence, just close enough to talk.

"Hey Roberta, how are you?"

Crossly, Roberta talks about her son. He promised he would take her to Italy, she says, but he forgot his promise. After she'd bought herself new dresses for the trip, she repeats, he forgot her. Nat knows they have a son who lives abroad whom they never see and hardly ever mention, but Roberta's speech doesn't sound all that logical.

"He got lost on El Glauco," she says now. "He got lost there, when he was little, before he had a beard. He had grass on his face, instead of hair."

"That doesn't make much sense, Roberta."

The woman looks away, as if hoping to change the subject. "Who cares."

Her hair is damp; Joaquín has probably just washed it and sat Roberta on the porch for it to dry. It looks nice that way, tucked behind her ears. Nat tells her so.

"You look very pretty, Roberta."

"Why don't you come through and sit with me. I'm bored."

"I don't have time right now. But I'm sure your husband would be delighted to sit with you and chat. Tell him."

"Bah, he talks different. We never understand each other. Haven't you realized?"

"Realized what, Roberta?"

"That that man doesn't understand me."

"You mean your husband? Of course he understands you!"

"No way. Here, in this place, no one understands anybody else."

"Well, that happens everywhere."

"Happens more in La Escapa, much more. Haven't you noticed that nobody was born here? Everyone comes from outside. Everyone speaks a different language. English, French, German . . . Russian! Chinese!"

Nat laughs.

"How can that be, Roberta? We all speak the same language here."

The old woman tuts, waves her hand dismissively.

"Bah! You're so confused. See? You're not understanding me either."

She can't forget Andreas. Her yearning is still immense. Sometimes her breasts swell with desire, her whole body tingles at the mere memory. His features, however, have already begun to blur. She shuts her eyes and tries to hold them, and yet they melt away. The sense of loss is swiftly gaining ground over her memory. One night she dreams of him again, but he a different man, taller, more refined. In the dream, there is an oily calm in which she imerses herself to swim. She makes easy strokes, contemplating the shafts of sunlight that sift through the water, a riverbed's greenish cast, the silver glint of the rocks at the bottom. When she wakes, she thinks: no, that wasn't Andreas.

Another day, she thinks she sees him in the distance. The feeling is impossible to describe. Perhaps the closest thing would be like looking out a window and viewing a scene from another world. A world that is now remote, painful, and opaque. But wasn't that how it had always been: remote, painful, opaque? Yes, she thinks, but she was in it before; now she's outside.

She doesn't spy on him now—she would die if he ever caught her spying again!—but she observes his house from afar. The door is almost always closed—he used to leave it open—and the van is almost never outside. Where does he spend so much time?

An odd stillness surrounds his house, and is only altered by minute changes—the blinds up today, closed tomorrow, the wheelbarrow in a new spot, rainboots beside the door that disappear the next day—changes that demonstrate that Andreas is still alive. Somehow this fact surprises her, because she feels like he has already died.

What might he think about what happened, about everyone condemning her? Would he feel compassion? Or would he, like the others, believe she's guilty?

Everything has happened in a very short time. So short that she is astonished when she thinks about it. She opened a new tube of toothpaste when she arrived in La Escapa, a tube she has been using two or three times a day, and yet, almost a third is still left. It's incredible, she thinks: to be completely enlivened inside, shaken, spun around and around again, in less time than it takes to use up 125 milliliters of toothpaste.

One day, the Cottage gate is open. Nat gets over her reservations and goes to see how they are. The husband is by himself. He came to check on the house, he explains, and looks at her seriously, his expression closer to curiosity than reproach. He tells her that the girl is doing better, recovering. Nat asks if they are angry with her. When it's possible, she says, she would like to visit them. The girl and the mother, both. She wants to apologize in person. He thinks a while before he replies. He strokes his chin in reflection, a gesture Nat finds stilted. No, he says, they aren't angry with her. Carelessness was her only mistake. One can't go around adopting half-wild animals. Some risks cannot be tolerated, he repeats, and one doesn't have the right to take those risks without weighing the consequences. Nat would like to say that Sieso wasn't half-wild, that the man had liked him, that she even saw him petting Sieso once. She wishes she could defend herself, but she knows she has no right to a defense.

Looking at her, the neighbor's pupils oscillate slightly, as if scanning her. The truly painful thing for them, he continues, is that Nat didn't want the dog put down. They had lost a lot, their daughter had lost a lot, why had Nat refused to lose anything? She must understand it in those terms.

"But let's not talk out here. Come inside. It's cold."

Nat accepts, although once inside The Cottage, the subject of the dog doesn't come up again. As he goes about switching on lights and turning on the heater in the living room, he talks to her about other things. He describes the minutiae of his job. He manages an insurance company, but his plan is to break away and open his own office. Being his own boss would be the best, he says, it's the only way to never be denied a raise! He laughs at his joke and then asks her about her own projects. He doesn't listen to her answer. And he doesn't seem all that worried about his daughter, Nat thinks, since his conversation is relaxed and even he looks happy. Maybe he's not all that upset, here with the not entirely unattractive neighbor girl, whom he now has in the palm of his hand, thanks to the unpleasant affair with the dog.

He has her in the palm of his hand, Nat repeats to herself, or one of them is in the hands of the other, at least. There exists a possibility to buy and sell forgiveness, apology, a restoration of honor. He wields the power of the victim and because of that privilege, he is, perhaps, the only one who can intercede on her behalf. But in order to obtain that pardon, Nat must expiate her guilt, surrender something in return. Briefly, she delights in the idea. Why not? Wasn't that how her story began with Andreas, an exchange of goods? The neighbor clearly desires her. He has always desired her and now he can attain her easier than ever. Nat imagines him licking his chops, closing in on her like a wolf. She is suddenly overcome with disgust. Those lips, that body, his weight on top of her, the sterile touch emphasizing the remove from what she had, lost, and cannot manage to forget. It makes her want to puke.

The neighbor removes his jacket. Nat zips hers up, says goodbye, and leaves.

A spirit of harmony spreads through La Escapa, symbolized by the Christmas garlands the shop owners string on the trees, little lights that blink rhythmically, a reminder that the year is coming to an end and all must transform into citizens of goodwill. Now nobody turns their head when she walks past, there are no nasty looks or snubs, at least none that she notices. At the shop, the girl goes back to treating her naturally—if not quite the same as before—forgetting or pretending to forget what happened. The gypsies offer her a hound pup, assuring her the animal will never give her any trouble, but Nat rejects the offer, terrified at the very thought of giving it another try. Joaquín hints that she can come back to their house whenever she wants—looking at the floor, blushing when he says it. Even Píter apologizes. He didn't know how to handle the situation, he admits, he knows he let her down, but there'd been no easy solution, it was a hell of a dilemma.

Nat hopes that the return of the wife and the children next door will mean a return to normalcy, even if that normalcy is still a slippery thing. No transgressor can be absolved without receiving punishment first, but her break up with Andreas seems to have served that function for the inhabitants of La Escapa. Maybe they consider her expulsion from that state of inebriated happiness a harsh enough sentence. Would she be absolved, she wonders, if she was still wallowing like a sow with her lover, when the poor little girl still cries while having her dressings changed? Those, she believes, would be their words: *wallowing, sow*. Thanks to the fact that she has no lover with whom to wallow, Nat dares to come out of hiding.

She goes with Píter to Gordo's bar on Christmas Eve, where a few people have gathered for drinks. The night passes quickly; they eat heartily, joke, pop champagne, and sing carols. The girl from the shop gets drunk and dances on a keg, obscenely swinging her hips. Her father, also drunk, makes her get down, laughing his ass off. Nat feels like that night everything is allowed, everything is forgiven, even the old grudge between Gordo and the shop owner. And so she keeps an eye on the beaded curtain in the doorway, turning to look every time someone walks in. She is intoxicated with turbid hope, an effect of the alcohol. And what if Andreas comes? Her hearts races at the mere possibility. But Andreas does not come.

In the wee hours, confused and emotional, she exchanges goodbye hugs with the others, warm hugs in the cold night. On her way home, she is tempted to go by Andreas's. Just a quick look, from a distance, she tells herself, nothing wrong with a little peek. Will he or won't he be home? Will there be a light on? Will music be playing? Will he have company?

But when she turns onto his road, the dark silhouettes of the prickly-pears—sinister, threatening forms—make her turn back, like a warning.

*

She's returning from grocery shopping when she sees the neighbor woman in The Cottage doorway, watering the potted flowers. She stops in her tracks, laden with bags, palpitating. When she starts walking again, the air is such short supply that she can barely move forward. She knows she must go right over and say hello, but she advances slowly, discarding the words she must not utter, selecting more appropriate ones instead, all with the same care she used to take while translating, although now she doesn't know meaning of the original text.

The neighbor greets her with a smile, pretty in a mustard-colored sweater and wide-legged maternity pants, hair pulled back, gleaming cheekbones. Her attitude surprises Nat. That reception, she thinks, but she doesn't know how to finish the thought. That reception.

They exchange kisses on the cheek. Nat's voices breaks when she asks after the girl. The neighbor says she's doing much better. She calls the girl so Nat can see her and the child obediently emerges from the back of the house. Despite its length, the wound that bisects her cheek hasn't managed to disfigure the child's features, which are extremely delicate, still undefined. There are also a few smaller marks on her chin and neck. But it's her seriousness that is most striking. She looks at Nat with expressionless eyes.

"They told us that the scars will barely be noticeable with time," the mother explains. "The lucky thing about being a child. The skin regenerates wonderfully."

Nat tears up. She apologizes to both of them. If only she could turn back time, she says. She is so terribly sorry for the damage she caused. So terribly sorry, she repeats. The girl is unmoved. The neighbor puts a reassuring hand on her arm, steps aside so Nat can come in. Nat enters their house, still holding her bags. Bewildered, she sits where she is told, looks around for the husband, the little boy.

"They're not here," the neighbor says. Nat hasn't asked.

Then she offers her coffee. While she prepares it in the kitchen, the girl remains at Nat's side, standing in silence. She has the lost look of children without a past; her eyes, more than the scars, now mark the existence of a before and after, a glitch in time. Nat tries to chat with her, but the girl answers in monosyllables. The child's own verdict, set in stone, is consolidated in her expression. She has read Nat her sentence, and it is not favorable.

"She's very introverted," the neighbor says when she returns.

They talk about her pregnancy, about Christmas. How was the Christmas Eve party? Did they have fun at Gordo's? They had to be with their families, obviously—her parents and his mother—the grandparents miss the grandchildren, but now, these days, she feels like retiring to the countryside, she's planning a little outing, Nat can come if she wants. Nat is uncomfortable. What is the meaning of this kindness? She has trouble chatting as if nothing's happened, but she thinks it is what they expect of her, and she must try. Now the neighbor is talking about costs. The cost of doing the renovations—the pool project, but also the kitchen, which has to be completely redone—plus Christmas presents, heating, medical expenses . . .

161

Nat catches on. It hadn't even occurred to her. She isn't sure if the woman said it in passing or purposefully slipped it into the conversation, but she swallows and asks:

"Was it . . . a lot of money?"

Oh, no, the neighbor hurries to explain. She means the pregnancy expenses. She sees a very prestigious OB-GYN, the same one who did her other deliveries, one mustn't skimp on some things. The girl's treatment was covered by insurance. Fortunately, she adds, Nat doesn't have anything to worry about. The past is in the past. She comes closer, leans in a bit, and lowers her voice. As she speaks, she traces the rim of her mug with a fingertip, taking the time to enunciate each word.

"Look, if we'd wanted to fuck you over, we would have reported you."

Nat freezes, unable to react. That abrupt manner of speaking is like a backhand across her face.

"What?"

"Report you. I'm saying we could have reported you. And we didn't. If we had wanted to fuck you over, fuck you over good, we would have done it, because you had everything to lose. So, as you can see, it's not our intention to get you back. You can relax."

Baffled, Nat nods. She can't interpret whether the neighbor's smile disarms or accentuates the aggressiveness of her words: a tight smile exposing her magnificent teeth. Her eyes move to the girl, who has sat down on the floor, in a corner. She's playing a video game, supposedly cut off but—it seems to Nat—not missing a beat of the conversation. The neighbor changes the subject, her smile softens almost imperceptibly, and now she talks about her husband. He went to the grocery store in Petacas, she explains, it's getting harder to find what you need in the shop. What she said just a few minutes before now seems like the product of Nat's imagination, and yet she knows it's not, it had been a piece of the staging all along: a meticulously studied script, performed line by line. Nat no longer hears, she wants to get out of there, she doesn't know how to end it. The neighbor rambles on, leaning back in her armchair. Occasionally, the girl looks up from her device, examines them seriously, and returns to her game. An excuse occurs to Nat. The heater, she murmurs. She left the heater plugged in. She better get going, she adds, it's an old model, it could catch fire any minute.

At the door, the neighbor takes her by the shoulder. This time she says Andreas, not *the German*, like she used to call him. Andreas, point-blank.

"I'm glad he left you."

Her eyes gleam as she says it. Nat wants to protest, wants to ask where she got her information, but she limits herself to a smile. The stupid smile of a clown, she thinks: the girl's injury gives her mother the legitimacy to act like this, the right to keep assaulting her, like someone bursting into another person's home. Andreas is a dark man, the woman tells her, manipulative and dirty. She knows him very well. Very well, she repeats, and those two words grow large, they contain a whole language, a whole private, secret world to which Nat has lost access. Nat could remind the woman that she'd said just the opposite once, that she hardly knew him. She could ask for details, she could stay and try to understand. But the desire to flee, to get away, prevails. She grabs her bags, smiles again, and leaves without a backward glance.

As she puts the groceries away in the fridge, she finds several broken eggs and two yogurt containers, open and empty. When had that happened? Who did it? She doesn't recall having left the bags unattended for even a minute. That—the broken eggs and empty yogurts—disturbs her more than the rest of the scene.

The landlord turns up on December 30th in a bad mood. The first thing he tells her, muttering at the floor, is that they've charged him double the usual price for a baby goat. They take advantage of everybody—idiots, all of them—who want something special for dinner on New Year's Eve, he's sick of their nerve. Sick, he repeats. Nat feigns indifference and goes to get the money. Who cares if it's New Year's, the landlord says, taking a seat on the couch. If it were up to him, they'd eat a kettle of chips and drink a few liters of beer, period. But the women, he says, they're the ones who complicate everything, their zeal for celebrating special dates, anniversaries and birthdays, showing off with their dishes, as if the food wouldn't be shat out in the end anyway. He wipes spittle on his sleeve, gives Nat a lengthy, mocking smile, and asks about the dog.

"Guess he was a real dud, eh?" he laughs.

It was her fault, he says, for not knowing how to handle him. Dogs aren't that complicated, they just need a firm hand. She spoiled him with her whims, with that nonsense of bringing him to the vet—or does she think he doesn't know about that? Whims on the one hand, and on the other, that obsession with tying him to the stake. Not surprising the dog went nuts. In any case, it's too late for regrets, every dog has his day. Still seated, he digs around in his pocket and hands her the bills, folded and wrinkled.

Nat does her calculations, gives him the money. Leery, he takes his time counting the bills. He stands up to observe her, legs spread, fists on his hips. She holds his stare until she buckles and lowers her eyes.

"And what are you going to do here now?"

Nat doesn't answer. She just wants him to leave.

"Now that you're not screwing anybody, I mean, what are you doing here?"

Something pops inside her. Like a sack of cold gel that spreads through each one of her limbs and extremities, weakening her muscles, annihilating her. She steps backward.

"Or maybe you are screwing somebody. When there isn't one, there's always another. Isn't that right? Anybody will do."

He comes closer. Nat backs up until she is against the edge of the table. She tries to scuttle farther away, but he holds her by the arm.

"Come here," he whispers. "Don't you want me to give you a little something too?"

Nat wants to cry out but her terror prevents it. Before she can make a sound, he claps a hand over her mouth as the other grips her arm even harder. He puts his head against hers, whispers in her ear.

"Don't scream. Nobody is coming to help you."

She tries to get him off her, pushes at him as hard as she can, but the landlord shows surprising resistance, trapping her, pressing her, his sweaty, enraged body, hard, stinking, controlling her, slamming her into the wall, twisting her arm as he commands her to shut her mouth, threatening to tie her up and gag her if she doesn't behave.

"Come on," he says. "Don't be a prude. You fucked the German and the hippie. You fucked your neighbor, maybe you even fucked the old man whose house you clean. Do I deserve any less?"

Holding her against the wall, he grabs her by the hair, forcing her head back. She feels a wrench of pain, his saliva on her neck, on her breasts, his growl as he subdues her. She shouts, but what leaves her covered mouth is not a cry for help: her strangled voice, stripped of its humanness, is the squawk of a bird before slaughter. He pulls her even more tightly, crushing her with his weight. Then he steps back, spits to one side, and laughs loudly.

"You're in luck girl. Suddenly, I'm not in the mood."

Nat contains her retching. At last she screams. She shouts that she'll call the police, she's going to report him, she'll tell everyone what he's done.

"Oh yeah? Will you tell your neighbors? Think they'll come to your defense? Why do you think I'm here?"

Sore, taken aback, Nat cries, rubbing her neck and bruised arm. She orders him to leave.

"'Course I'm leaving. Didn't think I was going to rape you, did you?"

Then he says that she makes him sick. He'd choose any woman over her. A she-goat, a cow. Always acting the little lady, he says. With those flat tits and that bean face. Go ahead, report him if she dares. No one will believe her, there are no witnesses. If she calls the police on him, her neighbors will do the same to her. Or did she think the matter of the dog was closed? They could still report her if they felt like it. She can go ahead and do what she wants. She shouldn't complain so much

He runs two fingers—the middle and index fingers together, held stiff—along the edge of the table as he stares her straight in the eye. That touch lingers even after he's already outside, starting the Jeep, and even a little later, coagulating in the air.

Nat does not call the police. She doesn't call anyone. She sits on the floor and drinks straight from a bottle of whiskey Píter brought one day. She seeks respite in numbness. But the roots of her hair still hurt from being yanked. And spasms wrack her hands.

Sharp pain is piercing her brain when she wakes. Daylight is a injury to her eyes. How long has she slept? She blinks hard, once, twice, several times, becoming aware of the room, the moment, and herself. She stumbles to her feet, tripping on the furniture. She sees herself from the outside, from a position of false calm, like someone filming her, an extra, a gatecrasher, the most insignificant role that could be assigned in a fictitious world—a set made of plastic, of cardboard. She drinks greedily but the water does not quench her thirst. She speaks out loud to clear the huskiness in her voice. Coughs. Her throat stings. It's cold.

She puts on her winter jacket and goes outside. The sun is already high in the sky, but it provides no warmth. More fakery, she thinks. A painted sun, garbage. The sky is stretched taut over El Glauco, the road stretches before her, marking the direction she must take.

Andreas's van isn't outside, but this time Nat doesn't stop to spy from a distance. She goes up to the house and sits beside the front door. She stays there for several hours, indifferent to whether the others can see her, indifferent to what they say about her, the rumors they spread, the accusations she receives or the offenses they allege, and absolutely indifferent to her dignity—or what, in other times, she would have called dignity but is now just an elusive term. She pees outside, in the bushes. She snuggles into her coat, reclines as best she can, dozes on and off.

She spends the whole day on the doorstep.

On the edge of night, the sound of an engine plucks her from her torpor. She sees the van first and then Andreas, getting out. She stands, smooths her hair. He looks at her wordlessly. Unmistakably severe. She has trouble recognizing him. Was that what his eyes were like? His body? Wasn't he a little taller, or shorter, maybe? So hunched, so thin? She goes to him and lays the palm of her hand on his chest, no pressure, hardly grazing it at all, an acknowledgment. Beneath the fabric, Andreas's skin releases a gentle heat, real and undeniable. But even that warmth doesn't remove her from the stage set, from the sense that none of this is real.

"Why did you come?"

"I don't know."

It's true: she doesn't know.

He observes her with curiosity. He looks closely at her bruised neck. Maybe he can guess.

"You don't look so good," he says. "Come on, come inside."

The house retains the warmth and smell of firewood. Nat sits on the couch and looks around in the half-dark, floundering in the strange mix of recognition and unfamiliarity. Li comes over, purring, rubs against her leg. Now they are both confused: Nat is unsure of her next step and Andreas clearly expects something from her, expects her to say or do something: why else is she there?

But it's evident that Nat has nothing to say to him. She studies him carefully, as if studying a stranger, while he takes a pack of cigarettes from his pocket, lights one, and smokes in silence. Who is that man? Why has she spent hours on his doorstep, waiting for him? What was the point, now that a paralyzing chill has settled within her?

Months ago, he asked if he could be inside for a little while. Now it's like she is asking it of him, though in a different way. The man before her had ignited something inside her, something big and unknown, labyrinthine and inexhaustible, yet she feels nothing. In Andreas's eyes, a message once flickered, a message she interpreted as access to a power or insight beyond others' reach. But that is gone.

Maybe she had gotten carried away by greed, the selfish urge to snatch more than what was hers to take. Maybe it was true and she was ungrateful. She had touched God, and still, it hadn't seemed enough.

Andreas breaks the silence. Calmly, passionless. He knows about everything that's been going on lately. Everything? Nat asks. Yeah, everything. But she'll get through it, he assures her. She shouldn't torture herself over what people say. Nat feels the weight of distance in his words.

"You know? I had to go to Cárdenas recently. Armed cops in the streets. Everything cordoned off, helicopters circling. They were waiting for somebody important, a prime minister, I think, a head of state or something, for some international summit. I didn't wait to find out, I left as soon as I could. A horror show."

Nat doesn't react. She doesn't understand what Andreas is saying. What is he talking about? Is he trying to comfort her, or warn her about a danger? Is there a hidden message in his words? Or is he just trying to take her mind off things? He sounds artificial, as if someone else was speaking for him, or through him.

In truth, he sounds ridiculous, clumsy, uneducated, just like he had seemed to her at first, when she saw him from afar and he was just a piece of the landscape, nothing more. The German, an ordinary man, a man like any other. And she, Nat thinks, she had been set on translating him, on bringing him to her territory. What an absurd ambition. It would be funny if it wasn't so ludicrous.

"What are you laughing at now?" he asks, stunned. "I just don't get you at all."

She considers staying, for a time. But the opposite urge—to leave—weighs on her as well. She has nothing to prove. She isn't looking to challenge anybody or draw attention to herself. But she wants to finish what she started and left only half-complete. She doesn't want to give up. The translations of the theater pieces, for example. Among other things.

Eventually, she decides to go live in a town nearby. She rents a very old house for less than what the landlord in La Escapa charged her. She washes the floors, scrubs the stove burners, sweeps and rakes, varnishes old wood, scrapes tile smooth, prunes dead branches: she doesn't consider it stagnation, the repetition of these same chores in a new place; instead, it reflects progress. Every now and then Píter comes to see her, brings her gifts, is as attentive as he was at the beginning, if not more so. His attentions no longer bother her. The two of them, she thinks, are more alike than she thought. Píter, at least, talks.

She feels invincible, beyond judgement, but her immunity comes from having lived, for a time, as if she'd tripped on a broken step while climbing a never-ending staircase and fallen into a void, while everyone else kept climbing, higher and higher, never noticing.

When she thinks about Andreas, something still twists in her gut, like a hangover. Often, she closes her eyes and takes solace in the memory of his hands running down her sides. The first touch of his fingers on her waist. The T-shirt that accentuated the rest of her nakedness. The darkness silhouetting the shape of their bodies. The plink of raindrops on the metal roof. She thinks about how a single instant—that instant, for example—is enough to justify an entire life: there are people who never had even that. But other memories have lost their substance. She discards them one by one, until she is left with nothing except that first day.

Her memory has shrunk. Her memory is now so small that she can fit it in her fist. Sentimental relics, she tells herself, do not deserve eternity.

One day she takes the car and returns to La Escapa. She drives up El Glauco and parks at the lookout point where Andreas left the van when they went together. She follows their exact route, not to salvage the same emotions, but to erase them and write new ones on top.

From her seat on a rock, she admires the scenery, the glassy film cast by the clouds, the wash of diluted color. She takes a slow in-breath. The chill air clears her sinuses, stings a little. Without having planned it, she composes an impromptu, private farewell.

She feels a tickle on her hand, an ant. She discovers a line of them marching across the rock where she sits, a disciplined line except for the specimen that has crawled over to her hand: the wayward one, the renegade.

She observes the ants closely. It's hard for her to reconcile the broad view from the top of El Glauco with that narrow universe: the big and the small, all together on the same mental plane.

She reaches a kind of peace, a revelation. Unexpectedly, the theft she committed in the past acquires its full meaning. She knows how to read it now.

She realizes you don't hit your mark through careful aim, but haphazardly, by way of deviations and detours.

She sees clearly how everything has led to this precise moment. Even that which didn't seem to be leading anywhere at all.

SARA MESA is the author of ten works of fiction, including *Scar* (winner of the Ojo Critico Prize), *Four by Four* (a finalist for the Herralde Prize), *An Invisible Fire* (winner of the Premio Málaga de Novela), *Among the Hedges*, *Un amor*, which was named by several Spanish newspapers as the book of the year for 2020, and, most recently, *La familia*. Her works have been translated into more than ten different languages, and she has been widely praised for her concise, sharp writing style.

KATIE WHITTEMORE translates from the Spanish. Her full-length translations include works by Sara Mesa, Javier Serena, Aroa Moreno Durán, Lara Moreno, Nuria Labari, and Katixa Agirre. Forthcoming translations include novels by Jon Bilbao, Juan Gómez Bárcena, Almudena Sánchez, Aliocha Coll, and Pilar Adón. She received an NEA Translation Fellowship in 2022 to translate Moreno's *In Case We Lose Power*.